THE
HAUNTING
OF
NATHANIEL WOLFE

THE HAUNTING OF
NATHANIEL WOLFE

BRIAN KEANEY

ORCHARD BOOKS
338 Euston Road, London NW1 3BH
Orchard Books Australia
Level 17/207 Kent Street, Sydney, NSW 2000

First published in 2008 by Orchard Books
A paperback original
Text © Brian Keaney 2008

ISBN 978 1 84616 520 7

A CIP catalogue record for this book is
available from the British Library.

1 3 5 7 9 10 8 6 4 2

Printed in Great Britain by
CPI Cox & Wyman, Reading, RG1 8EX

Orchard Books is a division of Hachette Children's Books,
an Hachette Livre UK company.

www.hachettelivre.co.uk

CONTENTS

1. Talking to the Dead 7
2. The Mug-Hunter 22
3. The Woman in White 32
4. Shallow Jack 46
5. Cat and Mouse 60
6. Below Stairs 73
7. Copperplate Handwriting 85
8. A Conspiracy Unmasked 99
9. An Accident in the Parlour 108
10. Listening at the Keyhole 117
11. The Oracle of the East End 126
12. The Layer-Out 143
13. Chiselling Charlie 162
14. William Monkton 168
15. Flown the Coop 180
16. Face to Face 190
17. Underground 196
18. A Very Important Person 208
19. Free and Easy 222

1. TALKING TO THE DEAD

It was a grimy March day and the smoke from hundreds of chimneys mingled its sooty breath with the mist that came drifting up from the river. By late afternoon the air had grown so thick it seemed to curdle in your lungs. People went about their business wrapped and muffled, coats buttoned up to their throats, scarves held over their mouths.

The fog transformed London. Instead of a lively, bustling city, it became a sinister and treacherous netherworld. People appeared out of the murky haze then disappeared again as it closed around them like a sea. Sounds were magnified in the gloom, even the steady chewing of a cab horse echoing dully in the lifeless air.

By seven o'clock it was dark and bone-chillingly cold. The line of people outside the William Wilberforce Memorial Hall in Wapping shivered as a full head of thick black hair. (Only Nathaniel knew about the special preparation his father purchased from the chemist to disguise the grey at his temples.) He was a strong man, built like a bull with a barrel chest and muscular arms. He wore a long, black top-coat and matching trousers, grey waistcoat, white shirt and stiff collar – the uniform of a professional man, a doctor perhaps, or a lawyer. The clear light of day would have revealed a certain shabbiness about his clothes, but in the pale yellow glow of the gas lamps, he looked eminently respectable.

'Ladies and gentlemen, welcome to an evening of hope,' he began. 'I say an evening of hope because that is what I bring. Like many of you, I know how cruel it is when a loved one is snatched away. I, too, have suffered such a loss.' When he said this he put his hand to his heart and lowered his eyes, as though feeling the pain of bereavement all over again. 'Believe me, ladies and gentlemen, after my own dear wife was taken from me I raged against heaven. But not any more. For I have discovered a sacred truth that I will share with you. It is this.' He paused, leaned forwards and in a stage whisper, added, 'The dead have not forsaken us. They are always among us. Even tonight, in this very room.'

There was a gasp from the audience as he said this and one or two of them craned their necks to look about them, as if they expected to see spirits hovering in the corners of the building.

'There is so much they are longing to say,' he continued in his normal voice, 'and tonight, through me, they will speak. That is my promise.'

He held them in the palm of his hand, as he always did. This was what he was good at. Not that it was difficult, for these were people who wanted to be convinced. Nevertheless, Cicero knew exactly what to say and when to say it. 'In a moment, ladies and gentlemen, I shall sit down on this chair and make myself available to those spirits who are here tonight. But before I do so, I must request that during the seance, there is complete silence. Remember, it is as difficult for the dead to break through as it is for us to hear them. We must all assist in the process by concentrating. Focus your minds on whomever you wish to speak to. Try to think of them as they were when they were hale and healthy, for that is how they are now on the other side. Let us begin.'

He sat down on the red velvet armchair in the middle of the stage. For a long time nothing happened and the expectation in the room grew deeper. Then suddenly his face began to change. He grimaced horribly like someone in the most appalling agony. His eyes rolled in his head and he slumped back in the chair like a dead man. A moment later he sat bolt upright again and began to speak. But not in the strong baritone voice with which he had introduced himself, for it was no longer Cicero Wolfe talking. 'I have a message for someone in the room,' he intoned in a thin quavering treble. 'Are you there, Elizabeth?'

A woman in the third row sprang to her feet. She was younger than most other people in the audience. The majority were elderly widows or widowers, but she looked no more than thirty. Yet grief had done its work on her features and she was certainly not out of place in such a company. 'Is that you, Jack?' she demanded, her voice trembling with emotion.

'Of course it's me.'

Nathaniel went over to the end of the row and signalled for her to come out. She looked stunned and moved like a sleepwalker as he led her up the steps and onto the stage. 'Ask him what his message is,' Nathaniel whispered.

'What do you want to say to me, Jack?' the woman asked.

'You must stop worrying about me, Elizabeth,' the spirit-voice continued. 'I am at peace now.'

The woman nodded, her eyes filling up with tears. 'Jack, what shall I say to Mr Mayhew?'

There was a moment's hesitation, then the voice

spoke again. 'What did I always say when I was alive?'

Elizabeth frowned. Then she nodded, eagerly. 'You said he loved nothing so much as the sound of his own voice. You said that for all his money he was just a great big windbag.'

'Exactly.'

'So you think I should turn him down, Jack?'

'You know what I think, Elizabeth.'

Elizabeth nodded. For the first time that evening she smiled and her face was transformed. Suddenly she looked young again. 'I'll tell him no, then.'

Nathaniel led Elizabeth back to her seat and a moment later another voice began to speak, thin and high – a woman's voice. 'Where is Gabriel?' it demanded.

A very tall, white-haired man with an enormous nose stood up at the back of the hall. 'I'm here, Lily,' he called out, excitedly.

Nathaniel led him up onto the stage where he stood as straight as a ramrod, despite his years. 'What is your message for me?' he demanded.

'Stop dwelling on the past, Gabriel,' Lily told him. 'You must concern yourself with the present.'

'But the boys won't speak to me any more, Lily. They've turned against me,' he complained.

'You know why that is, Gabriel.'

'I don't see why I should have to apologise.'

'You were always too proud, Gabriel.'

'So I have to go down on my knees to my own sons!' he continued, bitterly.

'You will have to leave your pride behind some day, Gabriel. There is no room for such things on the other side. Now is the time to make a start.'

Gabriel went back to his seat with his head bowed, looking a great deal more humble than when he had first walked onto the stage.

Nathaniel had to admit that Cicero was good. More than good. He was brilliant. If Nathaniel hadn't known otherwise, he might even have believed it himself. But it was all a fraud and Nathaniel was far from happy at his own part in the deception. Unfortunately, he had little choice. To say no to Cicero would have been to take his life in his hands – perhaps literally. Underneath the gentlemanly exterior, Cicero was entirely ruthless. He got his own way by bullying and if that didn't work, by violence – especially when he had a drop of gin inside him.

Ever since the death of his wife, Cicero had been inclined to take comfort in alcohol whenever things got difficult. That was what had brought about the end of his music-hall career – getting drunk, turning up late, forgetting his lines. When Nathaniel's mother

hearing their loved ones speak. The truth, Nathaniel strongly suspected, was that death meant the end of everything. You died, you were buried and your body rotted away into the earth. That was all there was to it. Everything else was just wishful thinking. You wouldn't catch him falling for nonsense like this.

At the end of the evening there were always people who were disappointed that their names had not been called since it wasn't possible for everyone to step up onto the stage. But even those who had waited in vain for a message went home with their faith in the next world confirmed. The only unbelievers who left the hall at the end of the evening were his father, himself and Mrs Gaunt.

Gaunt by name and gaunt by nature, the third party in the conspiracy was a thin, haggard-looking woman with sunken cheeks and long, bony fingers. If you had wanted a person to serve as an illustration of hunger, Mrs Gaunt would have done very nicely. She and Cicero had been cronies for a long time. Their connection went right back to the music-hall days when Mrs Gaunt had sometimes featured on the same bill as Henry and Louisa. In those days, incredible though it seemed to Nathaniel, she had been known as the Shadwell Nightingale. 'Her voice was as sweet as her face was sour.' That was Cicero's verdict on her, though never, of course, in her hearing.

Mrs Gaunt was present at every seance, mingling with the crowd as they milled about in the foyer, telling them confidences about herself, most of which were entirely untrue, and finding out little details about their lives in return. This information she passed on to Cicero when she slipped backstage just before the seance began.

After every performance, Mrs Gaunt left the hall with the rest of the audience, but a few hours later she turned up at the two shabby rooms Nathaniel and his father shared not far from the docks. By this time the money had been counted and she was there to collect her share. The landlady, Mrs Bizzantine, always opened the door to her but Mrs Gaunt showed herself upstairs. She knew the way well enough.

'Would you care to join me in a drop of gin Mrs Gaunt?' Cicero asked, though why he bothered with such pleasantries Nathaniel could not imagine, since the answer was always the same.

'I don't mind if I do, Mr Wolfe.'

They always addressed each other in these formal tones. It was never Agatha and Cicero, or even Agatha and Henry. Always Mrs Gaunt and Mr Wolfe.

Cicero poured some gin into a cracked cup and offered it to her.

'Thank you very kindly Mr Wolfe.'

Cicero raised his own, grimy cup. 'To the dead,' he said.

Mrs Gaunt chuckled and touched her cup to his. Then they both took a long sip of gin and sat back on their chairs with satisfied smiles.

Nathaniel knew what was coming next – it was always the same. They would begin to reminisce about their days in music hall, the artists they had known – all just names to Nathaniel – the occasions that had gone well and those that had not.

True to form, it was Mrs Gaunt who began. 'Do you know what I was thinking about on the way here, Mr Wolfe?' she asked.

'No, Mrs Gaunt. I do not,' Cicero replied.

'Archie Bennett. You remember him? He used to sing that song about two little orphans?'

Cicero nodded.

'I was remembering the time he fell over on the stage and broke his nose.'

Cicero grinned delightedly. 'Of course. He carried on to the end of the song, I believe. What a performer! My Louisa used to say, "it's people like Archie that keep the world turning".'

Nathaniel had heard this story many times before, including his mother's opinion of Archie Bennett. He decided to slip away and let them get drunk together. Outside a wind had sprung up, blowing away the fog and leaving a clear, cold March evening under a sky ablaze with stars. At first he set off without any real idea of where he was heading but pretty soon his steps began to lead him in a familiar direction.

He passed a big house which stood by itself, the last remnant of gentility in an area that was going steadily down in the world. Nathaniel let himself in at the gate and made his way to the front step where a tub of yellow flowers stood. He had no idea of their name, only that the sight of them blooming in March, when everything else was still locked in the grip of winter, made him feel hopeful. They weren't really the sort of flowers to put on a grave, being altogether too small, but he picked a few of them just the same. Whoever had planted them would be furious in the morning but Nathaniel could not help that. He needed to pay his respects and this was the only way he could afford to do so.

The churchyard of St Agnes the Martyr was kept locked at this time but it wasn't difficult to climb over the railings. He made his way to the corner of the churchyard and stood looking down at his mother's tombstone. There was just enough moonlight to read the inscription, though of course he knew the words by heart: *Sacred to the memory of Louisa Mary Wolfe, wife of Henry Wolfe, beloved daughter of William and Mary Monkton.*

The stone had been put there and paid for by his mother's parents, since at the time of her death his father could not afford one. Nor had his financial situation improved since then, any additional money he earned being immediately converted into gin.

Nathaniel had never met his maternal grandparents because of the great feud that had taken place in the family. They were respectable people and wealthy, too, at least according to Cicero. Mr and Mrs Moneybags, he called them. They had disapproved so violently of their daughter marrying a music-hall performer that neither party had ever spoken to each other again.

Nathaniel stood for a long time in front of the grave with his eyes closed, trying to recall his mother's face. It was she who had taught him his letters and he could clearly remember the sound of her voice as she sat on the floor beside him, drawing the shapes of the alphabet on a piece of slate and repeating their sounds out loud. But her features escaped him now. He had seen so many faces over the years. They rose up before his mind's eye in a great procession – a parade of those who had been left behind by the dead, just as he had himself. Such a long line of people that there was no room for his mother amongst their number. He sighed, opened his eyes and placed the flowers carefully on the ground. Then he turned and walked sadly away.

2. THE MUG-HUNTER

The pale winter sun shed very little warmth on the cobbled streets of Stepney but it was welcome all the same. Lily Campion was simply happy to be out and about for a change, getting some fresh air into her lungs – if you could ever truly call the air of London fresh. It made a change from slaving away indoors at the beck and call of everyone who needed something doing, from Mr Chesterfield himself to Mrs Simpson, the cook. As she walked along the street, a little boy rushed past her bowling a hoop as fast as he could with one hand, hanging on to his hat with the other and grinning all over his ragamuffin face. Watching him, Lily found herself echoing his delight. What a relief it was to be out of that gloomy old house where everyone went around with long faces, lowering their voices for fear of irritating the master.

This morning when Miss Sophie had handed over

a pair of boots that wanted re-soling, Lily could not help noticing that her young mistress's eyes were red from weeping. Not that there was anything unusual about that, for since her mother's death Miss Sophie was often to be found crying silently somewhere about the house, though never in her stepfather's presence of course. He had no patience with such displays of emotion.

She turned into Coulgate Street where the shoe repairer had his business and the buildings on either side of her immediately became shabbier and more neglected. She passed Mr Eisenberg's, the tailor. He made suits for underpaid, overworked clerks who spent their days laboriously copying documents late into the night in unheated offices all over the city. Beside his shop was Haverhill's the draper, where you could buy off-cuts and remnants that the big cloth merchants in the West End had sold off cheaply. Next door to Haverhill's was Mrs Jolly's fly-blown pie shop, where parcels of pastry and unspecified meat could be bought at three for a penny. Lily would not have eaten one of those pies if you'd paid her. She'd heard plenty of stories about where Mrs Jolly got her meat. Doubtless they were all highly exaggerated, but even if only part of what she had heard was true, no one in their senses would buy dinner from Mrs Jolly.

In the old days Lily would never have been expected to deal with a tradesman who had his business in a street like this. A respectable family ought to keep respectable company, in her opinion, and that included the tradespeople they dealt with. But the old days were over and done with now. Mr Chesterfield believed in looking after the pennies and if Miss Sophie wanted her boots repaired then the job had better be done as cheaply as possible. It wasn't Lily's place to pass any comment upon this and Miss Sophie certainly wasn't going to argue. She was far too much under her stepfather's thumb to even whisper her dissent.

Lily was still thinking about Mr Chesterfield's meanness when she found that she had arrived at the cobbler. She was just reaching into her basket for the boots when she felt herself hit in the back and pushed violently up against the door of the shop. She cried out in alarm. At the same time, she became aware that an unsavoury-looking young man was rummaging through the contents of her basket. An instant later his hand emerged clutching her purse and with a look of triumph he darted off down the street.

It took Lily a moment to recover from the shock but as soon as she came to her senses she was determined that the robber would not get away with her money. 'Stop thief!' she cried out, and she set off running after him as fast as her legs would carry her.

Nathaniel had just finished sticking a poster advertising his father's seances to the window of an empty shop further up the street when he heard Lily's cry. Looking up, he saw a man rushing headlong towards him while being pursued determinedly by a young girl. He had no difficulty working out what was going on. The man was Maggot Harris, a well-known street robber, or Mug-Hunter as people like him were popularly known. Nathaniel had often seen him on the streets and he was never very far from trouble.

Caution told him that he should not get involved. It was none of his business, after all. Things like this happened every day of the week all over the city. London was a dangerous place and you either kept your wits about you at all times, or you suffered the consequences. That was the law of the street. But even as he was telling himself this, some instinct seemed to overrule his better judgement, for just as Maggot Harris drew level, he stuck out his foot and tripped him. The Mug-Hunter gave a cry of dismay and went flying through the air, landing heavily on the pavement nearby and losing his grip on the purse. A moment later the girl came rushing up and snatched it back. She stood there, still panting but looking delighted with the result. Finally she said, 'Thank you very much.'

Nathaniel had no time to reply before Maggot Harris drew himself to his feet. His clothes were dusty, one trouser leg was torn, there was blood on his cheek and it was clear from the look on his face that he was bent on revenge. Immediately Nathaniel began to regret what he had done. Maggot Harris stepped towards him menacingly. Nathaniel was tall for his age but he was not yet thirteen and no match for the Mug-Hunter.

'So you want to be a little hero, do you?' Maggot Harris asked, sneeringly.

Nathaniel considered kicking out at him and making a run for it but he doubted very much whether tactics like that would work with someone as cunning as Maggot Harris. Instead, he opened his mouth to say that it was all a terrible mistake, that he hadn't meant to trip anyone up at all, but before he could speak Maggot Harris had grabbed him by his shirt front.

'Shut it!' Maggot told him.

Nathaniel swallowed his protest. He knew what was coming next and there was nothing he could do about it. He had been beaten before, of course. Plenty of times. When Cicero was in one of his drunken rages he could be utterly brutal, but

Maggot Harris was different to Cicero. It wasn't anger that motivated him. It was cruelty. He looked like the sort of person who enjoyed violence, as if hurting people was the only thing that really gave him pleasure. There was a light in his eyes now that told Nathaniel he had probably made the biggest mistake of his life. He cringed, waiting for the blow that would surely come, when suddenly, over Maggot's shoulder, like the answer to a prayer, he saw the unmistakable figure of Jeremiah Cumberbund coming down the street towards them. His spirits rose.

Jeremiah had a room in the same lodging house as Nathaniel and Cicero. He was a big man, in his forties, with a great beak of a nose and a thatch of reddish hair that stuck up on top of his head like a chimney brush. He was not a violent type, like Maggot Harris, but he was frightened of no one. He whistled as he walked towards them, his hands thrust into his pockets as if he hadn't a care in the world, which was probably true, for Jeremiah was a solitary individual. He had neither wife nor family and that, as he was inclined to tell anyone who listened, was the way he liked to keep things. 'No one to look out for but myself,' he would say. But despite this much-repeated maxim, he had always been kind to Nathaniel. Perhaps it was because Nathaniel did not shun him in the way that some people did.

For Jeremiah was a tosher. He earned his living in the underground labyrinth of London's sewers and, as Cicero was wont to observe, you could generally smell him before you saw him.

Never in his life before had Nathaniel been so pleased to see his fellow-lodger. He looked up gratefully as Jeremiah came to a halt, took his hands out of his pockets and tapped Maggot Harris gently on the shoulder.

Surprised, Maggot Harris turned round and regarded the newcomer doubtfully, his lip slowly curling in disgust as the unmistakable smell of the sewer began to steal over him.

'I'll thank you to let go of my friend, if it's all the same to you,' Jeremiah told him, speaking quietly but with the confidence of a man who knew how to handle himself.

'And what if it ain't all the same to me?' Maggot asked him.

'Then I'd say that it was your hard luck,' Jeremiah responded.

Maggot Harris hesitated. He looked Jeremiah up and down. Finally, he seemed to decide against provoking a confrontation with this strangely self-possessed individual. With great reluctance he let go of Nathaniel's shirt, but he continued to stare directly into his eyes. 'You needn't think I'm finished with you,' he muttered. 'Cos I ain't.' Then he spat on the ground before walking away with studied nonchalance.

Jeremiah stood and watched until the Mug-Hunter was out of sight. Then he grinned at Nathaniel, showing a row of broken teeth. 'Now that's what I call a thoroughly nasty piece of work,' he said. 'I should keep out of his way in future.'

'I intend to,' Nathaniel told him. 'Thanks a lot, Jeremiah.'

Jeremiah nodded. 'Well I'd better press on,' he said. 'There's always business to be done underground.' He tapped the side of his nose as he said this, then nodded at Lily and walked away, his hands thrust back in his pockets. A moment later he had resumed his familiar tuneless whistling.

'What did he mean by that?' Lily asked.

Nathaniel explained about Jeremiah's profession. 'A lot of people won't have anything to do with him,' he told her, 'but I've always found him to be a decent man if you treat him with respect. Anyway, I'd best be getting along myself. I've still got all these bills to put up.' He indicated the bag which he carried over his shoulder, still stuffed full of Cicero's posters along with a glue pot and brush. But he made no move to go.

'Well thanks ever so much for what you did just now,' Lily told him. 'You were very brave.'

Embarrassed, Nathaniel looked at the ground. He had felt anything but brave when Maggot Harris had taken hold of his shirt.

'My name's Lily, by the way,' she went on, sticking out her hand.

Nathaniel was a little taken aback at such formality but he took her hand and shook it. 'Nathaniel,' he told her.

'I'd have been in terrible trouble if I'd lost that purse,' Lily went on. 'It's not my money, you see. It's my master's. If I'd lost it he'd have taken it out of my wages.'

'That's hardly fair,' Nathaniel observed.

'Don't talk to me about fair!' Lily replied quickly. 'My master doesn't know what fair means. Still, moaning about it won't help, I suppose.' She regarded the poster Nathaniel had stuck on the shop front with curiosity. 'What's all this about then?' she asked.

'Seances,' Nathaniel told her.

Lily looked blank.

'You know – talking to the dead, contacting spirits, that sort of thing. Here, take a poster.' He stuck one in her bag.

She regarded him sternly. 'You shouldn't go meddling with that sort of thing,' she said.

'There's no harm in it,' Nathaniel insisted.

Lily shook her head. 'Those of us who are lucky enough to be alive have got no cause to be mixing with the dead,' she replied, speaking slowly and clearly, as if she were talking to a child she had found playing with a box of matches. 'No cause whatsoever. Now I'll bid you good day.' And with that she turned and headed back once more in the direction of the shoe repairer.

3. THE WOMAN IN WHITE

The William Wilberforce Memorial Hall was preparing itself to spend another evening in communication with the spirit world. Nathaniel was sitting on his stool inside the door collecting the entrance fees while Mrs Gaunt was mingling with the new arrivals, telling them stories about her late husband Walter (although Nathaniel was certain he had heard his father say that she had never been married in her life) and drawing confidences from them in return. 'He never touched a drop of alcohol in his whole life,' Nathaniel heard her say to a thin, red-nosed woman who nodded earnestly in approval. 'To tell you the truth, no woman ever had a better husband than my Walter,' she went on. 'Agatha,' he used to say to me, 'there is no time for small-mindedness in this life. We have to live every day as if it will be our last. For none of us knows the hour or the day he may be called to meet his maker.'

'That is so very true,' the red-nosed woman replied in a surprisingly educated voice. 'You think your whole life is ahead of you, burning brightly like a candle, and then one day it is simply snuffed out.'

'Is it your husband you've come about?' Mrs Gaunt continued.

The woman nodded. 'My poor Albert,' she said, taking out a handkerchief and dabbing at her eye.

'Has it been long?' Mrs Gaunt asked, sympathetically.

'Seven years,' the woman told her. 'But it always seems to me as if it was only yesterday. I don't think I'll ever really come to terms with it.'

'Oh, I know,' Mrs Gaunt assured her. 'I feel exactly the same way. Sometimes I wake up in the morning and for a moment I expect to find my Walter lying there beside me in the bed. Then I remember he's gone.' She sighed deeply. 'You just have to keep going from day to day, managing as best as you can by yourself.'

The woman nodded sadly and Mrs Gaunt went on with her questioning, probing and nudging, coaxing and cajoling until she had drawn out every last scrap of information, before moving on to her next victim. He was a bald old gentleman with enormous ears that looked like the wings of some exotic creature, and a tremor that shook his body continually. He leaned on a stick and sniffed loudly from time to time. Nathaniel could hear him telling Mrs Gaunt about an accident that had taken place in a factory, but after a while his voice was lost in the general hubbub.

As each new customer entered the hall, Nathaniel made a pencil mark on a piece of paper beside him. When there were nine pencil marks he drew a horizontal line through them and began again. That way he could keep a check on how many people had arrived. When he had made two hundred and fifty marks, it was time to shut the doors and begin proceedings properly. Nathaniel rose from his stool, drew the bolts that secured the front doors at the top and bottom, then went to tell his father that everything was ready. On his way he glanced in Mrs Gaunt's direction and, catching her eye, he gave an almost imperceptible nod. Mrs Gaunt, who was in the middle of telling the man with the enormous ears that Walter used to read his prayer book for half an hour every night before going to bed, did not even pause in her anecdote. Nevertheless, Nathaniel was quite confident that she had seen him. Mrs Gaunt had not spent twenty years on the stage for nothing. She was a consummate professional.

At the back of the hall, a door led to a storeroom full of items that had been abandoned or neglected for one reason or another: broken chairs, piles of dusty old books, a crate of cups and saucers that did not match, several sacks of old clothes and a roll of ancient carpet. It was here that Cicero had established his dressing room. He sat on a rickety wooden bench regarding himself solemnly in a cracked mirror that was propped up against the wall.

'Full house,' Nathaniel told him.

Cicero nodded without taking his eyes from his reflection. As Nathaniel was about to leave, however, he suddenly said, in a deep and sombre voice, 'Regard not them that have familiar spirits.'

'I beg your pardon?' Nathaniel answered.

Cicero turned and considered him gravely. 'The Old Testament,' he replied. 'Leviticus, chapter nineteen, verse thirty-one. A very clear warning against meddling with the souls of those who have passed on, most people would say. And yet I cannot believe it really applies to me. After all, there are no such spirits amongst my acquaintances. Only promises and dreams, hopes and expectations. I bring comfort to my audience, nothing more sinister. Reassurance and consolation. What harm is there in that? What do you say, Nathaniel? Surely I am not to be threatened with eternal damnation for bringing solace to those who have been robbed of their lives' companions?'

Nathaniel did not know what to say. He had seen his father in moods like this before. A gloominess would come over him from time to time and he would begin to question the life he had made for himself. These self-doubts would often be followed by a bout of heavy drinking. Fortunately the arrival of Mrs Gaunt at that moment forestalled the need for comment.

Mrs Gaunt was looking pleased with herself. 'Talkative they were tonight, Mr Wolfe. Very talkative indeed. I've got plenty of information for you. All sorts of little titbits. Now let me see, where shall I begin?'

Nathaniel left them to it. He went back out into the hall and began shepherding the last members of the audience into their seats. In a little while they had all settled down and the hall was filled with the expectant hum that always preceded a performance. Mrs Gaunt would not return to the hall. That would only draw unnecessary attention to herself. Instead, she would leave by the rear entrance, reappearing back at the lodging house later that evening. In a few minutes his father would come out onto the stage and in preparation Nathaniel now turned down the knob which controlled the gas supply, gradually dimming the house lights. The audience immediately grew quiet and tense with expectation. When at last it seemed they could wait no longer, the curtains twitched and out stepped Cicero.

While his father shared with the audience the news that the dead were always with them, Nathaniel found himself thinking about the girl he had met when he had been sticking up posters earlier that day. He had taken an immediate liking to her, even though she had so obviously disapproved of his participation in seances. There was something about the way she had stuck her hand out and introduced herself that had appealed to him, a directness that he wasn't used to. And, of course, there was the fact that she had told him he was brave. Nathaniel knew it wasn't true. He had never been brave in his life, and looking into Maggot Harris's eyes that morning he had felt nothing but terror. He'd been perfectly ready to say that the whole thing had been an accident. But he wished it was true. He wished he was brave, brave enough at least to tell his father that he wasn't going to take part in any more of these elaborate deceptions, brave enough to make his own way in life; but he was twelve years old, he didn't have a penny to his name and the world was a merciless place if you only had yourself to rely upon.

While Nathaniel was thinking this, Cicero had sat down in his chair in the centre of the stage and now he was sunk deep into his fraudulent trance. Speaking in the tones of a middle-class gentleman, he announced that he had a message for a woman called Hermione. Immediately the red-nosed woman rose to her feet. Nathaniel got down from his stool and went up the aisle between the two blocks of seats, stopping at the end of her row and beckoning her forward.

Nathaniel wondered how people like this woman, who was so obviously educated, could be so stupid as to believe in such nonsense. Why should a spirit want to communicate with the living, anyway? What could they possibly want from us? If they survived at all – and Nathaniel had the gravest doubts about this – then surely they were past caring about the life they had left behind? Surely they had better things to think about in heaven, or on 'the other side' as Cicero preferred to describe it?

When the woman had stepped onto the stage, Cicero informed her that her late husband was concerned about a financial matter she had been considering. She opened her eyes wide in astonishment at this news. 'Am I making a mistake?' she enquired.

'Best not to be too hasty,' Cicero replied.

It was always the same things they wanted to know about: money, marriage, illness and whether their loved ones were waiting for them. Hermione was a bit more forceful than some of the others, however. She was determined to get a definite answer from Cicero. Should she go ahead with her investment or not? Finally Cicero opted for caution. 'Don't do it,' he told her. 'You will regret it bitterly if you do.' The woman seemed content, as if this was what she had really wanted to hear. But her curiosity was not yet satisfied. She wanted to hear details of what the spirit world was really like; were there seasons like there were on earth? Cicero shook his head. 'It is just as you would wish it to be, at all times,' he promised her.

'But does it ever rain?' she insisted.

'If that is what you wish for,' Cicero repeated.

After she had finally returned to her seat, Cicero began speaking in a north-country accent, declaring that he had a message for a gentleman named Samuel. Immediately the man with enormous ears struggled to his feet, leaning on his stick and sniffing violently.

Nathaniel waited for him to make his way shakily out into the aisle. Then he took his arm and led him up to the stage. However, as they reached the steps Nathaniel suddenly became aware that a profound change had come over the hall. Or perhaps it had just come over him – he couldn't be sure. He began to feel cold, terribly cold, as if he was standing on the top of a windswept cliff, looking out over a vast grey sea whose icy depths could never be fathomed. A person might sink beneath those foam-flecked waves and carry on sinking forever, down and down for the rest of time. That was the meaning of eternity, he suddenly realised. It was an endless feeling of the world dropping away from you, a nothingness so vast that an individual life was no more than a speck within it, like a candle burning in a cathedral. He had no idea where these thoughts were coming from, only that they seemed to have taken possession of his mind completely. He felt as though he was in the hall and yet not in the hall at the same time, as if he had stepped outside himself altogether, or rather as if someone had summoned his presence and he had no alternative but to pay the closest attention to that call.

But what was this summons? What did it mean? And where was it coming from? Suddenly Nathaniel knew. The source of that appeal to the innermost core of his being was up there on the stage. It was right beside his father – a shadow, a shape, blurred at first but becoming clearer with every passing moment until finally it was entirely manifest and he was looking at the figure of a woman, dressed in a long white robe. Her eyes were the palest blue that

Nathaniel could possibly imagine and they were fixed directly on him. His heart skipped a beat and with every fibre of his being he knew her for what she was: a ghost. Hers was a life that had departed its earthly body but was not yet prepared to release its grip on the world for ever. There was unfinished business she yet had to perform. He could see it in her eyes. That was the reason for her appearance here tonight and that was why, out of all the millions of individuals on the face of the planet, she had chosen him for her haunting.

The chill that she brought with her was unbearable. If he had been standing naked on a mountain of ice he could not have felt more cold. Clearly, the world on the other side of death was not a place of eternal fire, like the preachers loved to tell you; instead, it was a place that had never known warmth. There was no comfort in it, no softness and no pleasure, only a fierce determination to survive, to continue to exist and to make oneself known to the world, a burning desire to communicate some horrible truth, some awful news that must be understood. And Nathaniel was the one who had been chosen to hear it.

If only he could have moved, he would have turned on his heel and fled, running out of the hall, down the street, out of the city, anywhere at all so long as he could leave this dreadful woman behind. He did not want to hear her speak. He did not want to know her horrible secrets. But his body was no longer within his control. He was rooted to the spot. And now the woman's lips began to move. She seemed to be speaking and yet Nathaniel could make out no sounds. Instead, there was a noise like the rushing of a great wind in his ears, a roar from the end of the world that drowned out every other sound. There was anger in her face at his incomprehension. She wanted him to understand what she had to say. It was a message of the utmost importance and he had to listen. But the roaring grew louder and louder until it was like a great wave of sound that came toppling down upon him, overwhelming him completely, so that for a moment everything went black and it seemed that the end of his life had come.

When he could see again, the woman was gone. Everything else was exactly as it had been. Cicero was sitting in his place on the red velvet chair and the man with enormous ears was standing impatiently beside Nathaniel, waiting for his cue to walk up the stairs onto the stage.

'You may approach me,' Cicero intoned with a trace of irritation in his voice. The old man angrily shook off Nathaniel's paralysed grasp and stomped up the steps. Nathaniel stayed where he was, aware only that his legs were shaking so much they could barely support him and that his clothes were entirely drenched with sweat.

Cicero quickly recovered his composure. He began telling the man with enormous ears that a spirit was saying something to him about machinery. 'A workplace of some kind,' he ventured. 'In the north of England. Lancashire, I think.'

The old man sniffed and nodded eagerly. 'Yes, yes,' he muttered. 'That's it. You've got it. That's him. That's my brother, Freddy.' He banged the end of his stick on the stage, in encouragement.

Nathaniel waited until Cicero had finished leading the old man on, telling him that his brother had felt no pain when he died, that he was watching over him every day, that he was united with their mother and father and that they were all looking forward to the day when he would join them. Then he led the man back to his seat and waited for Cicero's next message. But he was moving like someone in a dream. In his mind he kept seeing the figure of the woman in white, and the moment when she had opened her mouth as if she was going to speak to him. What had she wanted to say? What had been the terrible news that she had been unable to make him understand?

The rest of that evening passed in a blur. Other

gullible individuals were led up to the stage and then back to their seats stuffed full of Cicero's carefully crafted platitudes, but Nathaniel paid no attention to their stories. His father spoke of life on the other side of the veil as if it was an altogether peaceful existence, a bit like wandering about in a public park on a mild spring day, listening to the birds singing and admiring the early daffodils. The audience nodded their heads enthusiastically as if this idyllic picture was exactly what they had expected. But they knew nothing whatsoever about it. Alone, of all the people in the room, Nathaniel had felt the chill wind that blew from eternity. He had seen the proof that there truly was a life after death, but it was a very far cry from what they imagined.

After the seance was over, when the last of the audience had departed, Cicero came over and glared at him. 'What the hell do you think you were doing tonight?' he demanded.

'What do you mean?' Nathaniel asked him, though he knew perfectly well what his father meant.

'Standing there like a statue holding on to that old fool with the ears like an elephant,' Cicero continued. 'What on earth came over you?'

For a moment Nathaniel considered telling him the truth. He imagined explaining that while his father had been standing up on the stage pretending to have dealings with the spirits of the dead, he, Nathaniel Wolfe, medium's assistant and jack-of-all-trades, had genuinely witnessed a ghostly manifestation. He wondered what his father would say to that. It would certainly give him something to think about. But he said nothing. His father would most probably have clipped him round the ear and told him not to act the fool. There was only room in his world for one visionary, and that was Cicero Wolfe.

4. SHALLOW JACK

Cicero said no more about the matter after that. He seemed lost in his own thoughts, and as they walked back together to their lodgings the same sombre mood that had come over him in the dressing room began to descend upon him. By the time they reached home it had resolved itself, just as Nathaniel had predicted, into a desire to get thoroughly and completely drunk. Cicero counted up the night's takings and gave Mrs Gaunt her share. Then the two of them set about finishing off whatever there was to drink in the house. Between them they consumed three quarters of a bottle of gin, but Cicero was far from satisfied. He stood in the middle of the room, stretching his arms above his head, like a man who has just got out of bed on a fine summer's morning and is looking forward to whatever the day may bring.

'I shall go forth from this place to a public house or common inn and mingle with my fellow man,' he announced in sonorous tones. 'Therein shall I find balm for my troubled soul. Come Mrs Gaunt, let the world do its worst. We two shall prove ready for it.' With these words he staggered unsteadily out of the room, followed by Mrs Gaunt grinning all over her face. She was well aware that in this mood Cicero would not know whether he was paying for one person's drinks or two.

Nathaniel was initially relieved to be left alone to think about his experience. It was the first opportunity he had had to try to make sense of what had happened to him earlier. But it was not very long before he began to grow uneasy in his solitude. Supposing the woman in white returned to visit him in his lodgings. Could she do that? Why not? Surely one address was just the same as any other to her? Spirits were not likely to be bound by geography. Anxiously, he got to his feet and paced up and down the room. The more he thought about it, the unhappier he felt. Finally he made up his mind to go downstairs and knock on Jeremiah's door.

Jeremiah did not look particularly surprised to see him. 'I heard your dad going out earlier,' he told Nathaniel after inviting him in. 'He sounded good and ready for a night on the tiles.'

'I think he was,' Nathaniel agreed.

There was very little in the way of furnishings in

Jeremiah's room, just a straw mattress in one corner, a couple of wooden boxes in which the tosher's meagre belongings were stowed, two wooden chairs and a small table on which there stood a candle stuck into the neck of a bottle. Beside it was a parcel wrapped in greasy brown paper. On the opposite side of the room from the mattress, a flat wooden cage with a wire grill at the front stood on the floor against the wall. It was full of rats. As soon as Nathaniel entered the room they began running back and forth feverishly, bumping into each other in their fury and looking out at him with eyes that seemed full of viciousness. Nathaniel glanced at them nervously.

'Don't you take any notice of them beauties,' Jeremiah told him. 'They've got no business with you, nor you with them. You just sit yourself down and they'll settle in time.'

Nathaniel sat down on one of the chairs and Jeremiah sat opposite him. 'I was just about to have a spot of dinner,' he informed Nathaniel, unwrapping the parcel, which turned out to contain a meat pie. Nathaniel eyed it with interest. For an extra shilling a week their landlady, Mrs Bizzantine (or Mrs Busybody, as Cicero preferred to call her) provided meals for her lodgers, but Cicero had dispensed with her services a long time ago, preferring instead to spend the extra shilling on gin.

Consequently, Nathaniel was forced to get his meals wherever he could, which meant that he often went for long periods without anything to eat at all.

Seeing his expression, Jeremiah broke the pie in half and offered it to his visitor. Nathaniel took it gratefully and sank his teeth into the pastry, relishing the crispness of its texture and the rich brown meat and gravy within. The two of them munched together in companionable silence for a time, while in the corner of the room the rats squealed with envy. When they had finished every last crumb, they licked their fingers and sighed in satisfaction. 'You can't beat one of Mrs Jolly's pies,' Jeremiah said.

Nathaniel nodded his agreement.

Jeremiah leaned back in his chair and considered the animals in the corner. 'How much do you think them rats are worth?' he asked, after a while.

Nathaniel shrugged. He couldn't imagine why anyone would want to pay anything for rats.

'One shilling and eight pence,' Jeremiah told him, a note of triumph in his voice.

Nathaniel looked at him in astonishment. It was more than a week's rent.

'I can see you don't believe me,' Jeremiah continued, 'but it's true. There's twenty of the little beauties in that cage. Twenty rats at a penny a rat makes one shilling and eight pence.'

'But who will pay a penny for a rat?' Nathaniel asked him.

'The landlord of the George and Dragon in Shadwell, that's who,' Jeremiah told him, 'on account of the fact that there's no end of fellows what will bring their dogs along on a Wednesday night and put them into the ring alongside the rats to see who can kill the most in the shortest time.'

Nathaniel nodded. He should have guessed as much.

'There's plenty more besides who'll wager money on the result,' Jeremiah continued. 'And the landlord of the George and Dragon is the one who keeps the books, *and* the one who holds the bets, *and* the one who makes the most money at the end of the night. In consequence of which he and I have a little understanding, you see.' Jeremiah tapped the end of his nose. It was one of his favourite gestures. 'There's no rat like a sewer rat when it comes to a bit of sport. If the dog ain't up to the mark, the rats will be all over him, I can tell you.'

Nathaniel had no difficulty in believing Jeremiah's description. He glanced nervously at the cage and the rats stared back at him malignantly.

'What do you say we step outside for a little while?' Jeremiah said, a moment later. 'I've a mind to smoke a pipe or two and look up at the stars.'

Nathaniel agreed. So they went and stood on the front porch, leaning against the railing while Jeremiah took out his clay pipe and filled it with tobacco. Unfortunately it was a cloudy night and there was not a star to be seen, but Nathaniel was not disappointed. He was happy enough to have left the rats behind.

'Your dad gets himself worked up into a proper lather from time to time,' Jeremiah observed, after he had got his pipe alight and puffed great clouds of blue-grey smoke out in front of them.

'Yes, he does,' Nathaniel agreed.

'No doubt it's on account of the nature of his work,' Jeremiah went on.

'Well yes, I suppose so,' Nathaniel conceded.

'Standing up in front of folks like that, making speeches and everything. It must take its toll on a man.'

'Perhaps.'

There was silence for a while. Then Nathaniel asked, 'Jeremiah, do you believe in spirits?'

Jeremiah's face took on a troubled expression. 'Well now, Nathaniel,' he said. 'I wouldn't want to imply any disrespect to your father.'

'No, of course not,' Nathaniel assured him. 'I realise that.'

'And I wouldn't want to contradict him, neither.

Seeing as how he's an educated man whereas I've had no learning whatsoever. But it's just that, never having seen one myself, I wouldn't like to say for definite one way or the other.'

'But if they do exist,' Nathaniel asked him, 'do you think they might want to harm us?'

Jeremiah took a long draught on his pipe and considered this question. As he blew out the smoke again, he nodded his head slowly. 'Well it has to be a possibility, Nathaniel,' he declared. 'I don't think anyone can dispute that. After all, not every living person you come across means you well. You know that yourself from bitter experience. That Maggot Harris for example – he'd happily cut your throat and sell the blood to the butcher if he'd buy it. Well, it stands to reason then that if there are such things as spirits – and I'm not saying there are or there ain't – but if there are, not every one of them is likely to have your best interests at heart neither, if you take my meaning.'

Nathaniel nodded. Jeremiah had expressed the very thoughts that were in his own mind.

'Mind you, I shouldn't go worrying your head about it, if I were you,' Jeremiah continued, sensing Nathaniel's growing anxiety. 'A lot of it is no more than jaw in my opinion. Now, down in the sewers there's a great deal of talk about spirits and the like.

Toshers is superstitious folk on the whole and there's plenty of them believes in a ghost what they call Shallow Jack.'

'Shallow Jack?' Nathaniel echoed.

'That's what they name him. They say he haunts the sewers under London. I know plenty of folk who'll swear blind they've seen him. Nothing you can say will convince them otherwise, and whenever someone goes missing – which does happen from time to time I can tell you, sewers being dangerous places – people will say that Shallow Jack has taken him.'

'Do you think it's true?' Nathaniel asked.

Jeremiah's pipe had extinguished itself. He knocked the contents out on the railing, took another plug of tobacco from his tin and busied himself with filling it. Only when the pipe was filled and lit once more did he venture a reply. 'The way I see it is this,' he began. 'Down there in the dark people gets tired and muddled. There's vapours and fumes that confuse the mind. You stay down there long enough and your imagination begins to play tricks on you. In my opinion that's all there is to it. People go missing underground because the sewers are treacherous places, even for those what know them. If you get caught down there when a storm breaks you could be drowned before you had a chance to get above ground. And if your body wasn't washed out to sea, then the rats wouldn't leave very much behind for folks to grieve over. You mark my words, Nathaniel, it's tricks of the mind that makes people see ghosts, and that's all there is to it.'

After a while it grew too cold to stand outside and talk. So they went back indoors, parting at Jeremiah's door, since Nathaniel did not particularly wish to pay the rats another visit. It was quite dark when he got back to his own lodgings and he groped around for a candle to light him to bed, but there was not even a stub to be found.

Cicero could only afford to rent two rooms from Mrs Bizzantine. One of them was used as their parlour. The other was the bedroom which Nathaniel shared with his father. Unlike the parlour, this latter room had the benefit of a window. It was not usually completely dark in there at night for there were no curtains, but tonight there was little or no moonlight outside and Nathaniel had to find his way to the bed by touch. He took his clothes off quickly and lay under the blanket shivering with cold. Although he had been determined to put it out of his mind, he immediately found himself thinking about the woman he had seen earlier that evening. He remembered again the terrible chill she had brought with her and he found himself returning over and over again to the same questions. Why had she chosen to appear to him? What did she want? Would she return?

He found it impossible to sleep. The slightest sound anywhere in the house made him jump. The creak of the stairs, the rattling of the windowpane, a door slamming below him – any of these noises made his heart stop with terror and the blood freeze in his veins. After a couple of hours lying rigid in his bed, however, he heard the unmistakable sounds of Cicero returning, stumbling about on the stairs and cursing loudly as he barked his shins on objects that other lodgers had left lying about. It took him a great deal of time and trouble to open the door of their rooms but at last he came blundering in like some great beast in its death throes. Somehow he made his way into the bedroom without bumping into anything further and there he collapsed on his bed in a drunken heap. Within minutes he was snoring loudly.

Oddly enough, his presence was a source of some relief to Nathaniel. Not that his father would have been any good if the woman in white had reappeared. He had been quite unable to see her the first time and no doubt the same would be true of any subsequent manifestations. Besides, nothing would wake him now, not for hours at least. If the last trump itself were to be blown and the Day of Judgement declared, Cicero would be unable to rise from his bed to meet his maker. He had drowned his uneasy conscience in gin and neither he nor it would resurface until the middle of the following morning.

Nevertheless, Nathaniel somehow felt easier with the knowledge that there was another person in the room and little by little he began to relax. In time he felt the first waves of sleep's peaceful current bearing him away from his troubles and he sank gratefully into oblivion.

He was woken by the sound of a woman's voice calling his name. Terrified, he sat up in bed. Had he imagined it? No, there it was again. It was the stillest hour of the night and the whole house was as dark and silent as the grave. Even Cicero was no longer snoring. Nathaniel sat perfectly still, not even daring to breathe. Had he really heard that voice, or had it just been the remnants of a dream lingering in his mind even after he had broken the surface of sleep? He listened with his whole body, expecting the summons to be repeated yet dreading to hear it. But silence continued to stretch away from him like the landscape of an unknown country.

He became aware that he was terribly cold and immediately he thought of the dreadful chill that had overcome him as he stood before the stage the previous afternoon. The woman was coming again, he felt certain of it. He waited for that terrible sense of emptiness to surround him, bracing himself for the world to drop away, leaving him to fall through the yawning nothingness that lay on the other side. But it did not happen, and gradually he realised that this coldness was altogether different from the cold of death. It was more substantial somehow, more solid, if that made any sense. As his eyes slowly grew accustomed to the darkness and he began to make out the shapes in the room, he realised that the window was open. How had that come about? He was certain it had been closed when he had got into bed. Could Cicero have opened it in the night? Surely not. He was too far gone to manage such an operation, and too drunk to care, anyway. Somebody else must have opened it. But there was no one else in the room. Or was there?

Again Nathaniel held his breath, listening for the slightest sound that might give away the presence of some other being. But there was nothing more than the sound of his own pulse hammering in his ears. For some strange reason he found himself remembering what the girl he had met in the street had told him. She had said that he was brave. She would not have made such a judgement if she had seen him now, too terrified to get out of his bed and close the window. She would have thought he was an utterly miserable specimen.

It was this thought that decided him. He would carry on like this no longer, he told himself. If there was someone else in the room, whether mortal or spirit, then let them show themselves. With his heart racing, he got out of bed and padded across the room towards the window. He expected to feel a ghostly hand touch him on the shoulder at any moment, but nothing happened. Summoning up every last scrap of his courage, he turned his back on the room, took hold of the sash and pulled it down, closing the window completely. Then he turned round, ran back across the room and jumped into bed. He felt a wave of relief roll over him. He had braved his fears and survived the experience. Perhaps it had been Cicero who opened the window after all, he told himself. In his drunken state he might have felt in need of air. Yes, that was probably it. He was getting himself frightened about nothing.

Then he remembered the voice. That had seemed real enough! 'Maybe I'm losing my reason,' he told himself, suddenly panicking again, 'taking leave of my senses. And if that's the case, then they'll carry me off to Bedlam as soon as they find out. But I won't tell anyone. I'm going to forget all about what happened at the seance, that's what I'm going to do.

It's nothing to worry about. I probably didn't have enough to eat all day and grew light-headed, what with traipsing about all over London putting up posters and then falling foul of Maggot Harris. It's enough to make anyone muddled and confused. I thought I saw something that wasn't there, that's all. It was only my mind playing tricks on me, like Jeremiah said. And now tonight I've had a bad dream and got myself worked up over nothing. I just need to calm down. There's no such thing as ghosts.' He repeated these assurances to himself over and over again, until the words seemed to blur together in his mind and he fell once more into the blissful ignorance of sleep.

5. CAT AND MOUSE

The bells of St Agnes the Martyr were chiming six o'clock when Nathaniel woke up the next morning. He looked out of the window at the ragged clouds chasing rapidly across the sky and the events of the previous night seemed little more than a dream. 'Letting your imagination run away with you, that's all it was,' he told himself, as he went downstairs and washed his face under the pump in the yard. 'You ought to be ashamed of yourself.'

There was nothing to be had for breakfast. Nor was there any money to buy food. If there had still been the price of a drop of gin in Cicero's pocket, he would not have been lying on his back in the bedroom right now, snoring loudly enough to wake the dead.

Except that the dead don't wake. They keep on sleeping. Only gullible people believed anything different. And whatever else Nathaniel was, he wasn't gullible. Poor, unschooled, shabbily dressed, and not always as clean as he might be – he was prepared to own up to all of these. But gullible he was not. That was the word for people who came to his father's seances, whereas Nathaniel Wolfe had seen things from the inside. He knew the tricks of the trade. If a person happened to be weak, they might be taken in. And all sorts of things could make you weak, like losing a loved one or not having enough to eat.

Well, there was something he could do about an empty belly. He could go and earn himself the money to buy some food. Billingsgate Market was the place. There were plenty of fish-sellers there prepared to pay two pence a day to a lad who was willing to bend his back unloading boxes of fish. Nathaniel knew several of them by name and they were decent enough fellows. They smelled a bit strongly of fish, of course, but that was all part and parcel of their calling.

'A man's stink is his badge of office.' That was what Jeremiah had remarked one morning after Cicero had come home from one of his drunken binges and begun complaining bitterly about his housemate's smell. He had not been home for four days and when he finally reappeared, looking very much the worse for wear, he had rounded on Jeremiah, who had been sitting on the doorstep, smoking his pipe and minding his own business.

'Good God, man!' Cicero had exclaimed, waving his hands about as if to dispel a cloud of imaginary flies. 'You smell like a dead dog that's been locked in a shed for a fortnight. I must speak to Mrs Bizzantine about this. It cannot continue. You are a hazard, sir. A danger to the public and a menace to the community.' Then he had pulled a grimy handkerchief from his pocket, clutched it to his mouth, and made his way up the stairs, coughing and spluttering.

Nathaniel had been sitting beside Jeremiah at the time and was so embarrassed he had scarcely known what to say. But Jeremiah had seemed entirely unperturbed. He merely puffed away at his pipe and brushed Nathaniel's apologies aside. 'Your dad don't mean no harm,' he said, good-naturedly. 'It's all hot air with him. Besides, there ain't nothing wrong with a good, honest stink. You can tell a man's calling by his odour and that's something to be proud of.'

Nathaniel wasn't sure he agreed with this, especially when the smell in question was fish. But he needed to eat. So he put on his coat and set off through the streets of Stepney, heading for London's biggest fish market.

It was strange to find these lanes and alleyways deserted when they were normally thronging with all sorts of people – street musicians and beggars, tinkers and scavengers, old clothes men and umbrella girls, barrow boys, fruit-sellers and pickpockets. Now there was only a blue-coated Peeler standing at the corner of Cable Street, stamping his feet against the cold. He eyed Nathaniel suspiciously but made no move to detain him.

Before very long Nathaniel came within sight of the Monument to the Great Fire that had burned most of London to the ground two hundred years earlier. A fence had been erected around the top of it to stop people throwing themselves off in order to escape debts that couldn't be paid or a broken heart that couldn't be mended.

Now the seaweedy smell of the market began to steal over him and within minutes he had caught up with the crowd. The whole length of Lower Thames Street was lined with carts pulled by horses and donkeys. Those who could not afford to keep an animal pushed barrows before them. Ragged-looking boys and girls carried baskets on their heads. They were streetsellers, every one of them, on their way to buy their stock, and all making for Billingsgate as fast as they could go, lest someone else should get the fish more cheaply. Nathaniel joined the crowd, making his way beside the Thames, where a forest of masts had sprouted overnight as lines of fishing smacks queued, one behind the other, waiting for the opportunity to land their silvery cargoes.

At last he came upon the market itself, a great barn-like building surrounded by a pillared colonnade. Gaslights were burning at every stall and the business of buying and selling was being carried on with a great deal of noise and bustle. Each stall specialised in its own particular kind of fish and stallholders tried to drown each other's voices as they called out their wares. 'Handsome cod, best in the Market!' cried one. 'Yarmouth Bloaters, who wants 'em?' yelled another. They held up buckets of shrimps, jars of oysters and crates of wriggling eels.

Nathaniel pushed his way through the crowds, looking for a red-faced man known as One-Eyed Harry on account of having lost an eye in a fight with another stallholder many years earlier. In those days Harry had been ready to come to blows with anyone whom he suspected of cheating him. But nowadays he was bent over with arthritis and more than ready to pay for a little help lifting boxes of fish.

He grinned when he saw Nathaniel. 'You've turned up just in time,' he said, and immediately sent him down to the wharf to fetch two boxes of turbot.

Boxes of fish are a great deal heavier than most people would imagine, and by the time Nathaniel had been back and forth to the wharf another dozen times that morning, his legs were almost ready to give way underneath him. Fortunately, One-Eyed Harry took pity on him. 'You look worse than I do,' he told Nathaniel. 'Here, go home and get yourself something to eat.' He handed Nathaniel two pennies, even though he had only done half a day's work.

Nathaniel took the money gratefully and made his way out of the market. There were plenty of barrow boys nearby selling penny loaves and spiced cakes. But Nathaniel knew better than to waste his money on Billingsgate Chaff, as it was called. It was all made for those who had come a long way and were desperate for some sustenance. The flour was only sweepings, mixed with anything the baker could get hold of, even sawdust. Better bread could be bought for the same money closer to home. So he forced himself to walk past them all, ignoring the smell that teased his nostrils almost beyond endurance, and began to retrace his steps towards home.

He was nearly within sight of Mrs Miggins' Baker's Shop, where the best loaves in the whole of the East End were baked, when he saw something that made him stop in his tracks. Standing on the corner of the street talking to a tall, dark-haired man with a scar on his cheek was Maggot Harris. The dark-haired man was dressed like a gentleman, though what any gentleman would be doing talking to Maggot Harris was hard to understand.

Nathaniel was just about to disappear as

quickly as possible in the opposite direction when Maggot Harris looked up and caught sight of him. His eyes lit up with malice. He nodded farewell to the scar-faced gentleman and began to make his way briskly towards Nathaniel.

Nathaniel turned and fled. But Maggot's legs were long and he hadn't spent the morning working on an empty belly. However much Nathaniel twisted and turned, weaving his way between buildings and dodging under archways, Maggot stayed right behind him.

Nathaniel came out of a passage between a public house and a butcher's shop just as a hansom cab rumbled past. With a cry of glee, he jumped onto the running board and waved with delight as Maggot stood, hands on hips, watching him being carried speedily away. But the cabby wasn't having any street urchin hanging on to his cab. He struck out viciously with his whip, catching his unwanted passenger across the face.

Nathaniel cried out in pain and lost his grip on the cab, falling heavily onto the cobbled street and rolling into a pile of newly deposited horse dung. When he had got to his feet and brushed off the worst of it, he looked up to see Maggot Harris running full-pelt down the road towards him. Cursing to himself, Nathaniel ducked down the nearest alleyway, only to find that his sense of direction had deserted him. He had reached a dead end. He turned and saw the silhouette of Maggot Harris at the entrance to the alley. He had come to a halt and was walking slowly towards Nathaniel, smiling cruelly.

'I've got you cornered now,' Maggot said.

Nathaniel turned and made a leap at the wall. He got his hands on the top and began pulling himself up. It took all his strength but at last he was over. On the other side was a courtyard where three old women were sitting on a bench washing clothes in a tub. They stared at Nathaniel in amazement. The biggest of the three – a woman with a huge bosom and a mane of chestnut hair – stood up and advanced towards him threateningly. 'Oi! What do you think you're doing?' she demanded. But there was no time for explanations. He dodged past her, threw himself at the opposite wall and began scrambling over. As he did so, he caught sight of Maggot Harris jumping down into the courtyard. Quickly Nathaniel dropped down the other side of the wall into a narrow passageway and set off running once more.

The urge to give up was growing in him. A voice in his head kept telling him that he could never out-run Maggot Harris, that he should just accept his beating and be done with it. But in another part of his mind he knew very well that Maggot Harris might not be content with a beating. Life was cheap in the great metropolis of London, and what was one young boy more or less to its citizens? People were found murdered every week of the year, their throats slit, their bodies tossed into the Thames. And the perpetrators were seldom caught. They slipped away into the underworld. Yet everyone knew who they were – people like Maggot Harris.

At the end of the alleyway was a church. In desperation Nathaniel pushed open the doors and stepped inside. He ran halfway up the aisle and hid behind one of the pews. It wasn't a very good hiding place but he knew he could run no longer. And surely even someone as unscrupulous as Maggot Harris would hesitate to attack him in a church? But even as he thought this, the sound of the door banging shut echoed hollowly throughout the building and he knew Maggot had followed him in.

Nathaniel peeped cautiously out from under the pew. He could see Maggot standing in the shadows just inside the door, looking all around.

'I know you're in here somewhere,' Maggot called out. 'And when I find you, gawd help you, 'cos no one else is going to.'

Now he began making his way slowly and deliberately up the central aisle and it was only a matter of time before he would reach the place where Nathaniel was hiding. Nathaniel began shuffling backwards along the row towards the outside aisle, but even though he moved as quietly as possible, the noise was enough to alert Maggot. He quickened his pace but just as he was about to pounce, a figure emerged from the shadows.

'Can I help you?' the vicar asked.

Maggot looked at him in confusion. 'I was just... I mean I just popped in, to say a prayer, like...' he muttered unconvincingly.

'I'm afraid the church is just about to close,' the vicar went on. 'Perhaps you'd like to come back another time?'

'Oh yeah. I'll do that,' Maggot said, looking ominously in Nathaniel's direction. 'I'll come back another time,' he added, speaking slowly and deliberately in case Nathaniel had any doubts about his intentions.

'I'll lock the door behind you then,' the vicar went on, as if he hadn't noticed the threat in Maggot's voice.

Reluctantly, Maggot allowed himself to be led down the aisle and out of the church. When he had gone the vicar bolted the door firmly behind him. Then he turned to face the pews.

'You can come out now,' he declared.

Nathaniel stood up.

'Thank you, sir,' he said.

'Thank the Lord, young man,' the vicar went on. 'I am merely his servant. Now, since our friend outside will no doubt be waiting not very far away for you to re-emerge, I suggest you make your exit through the vestry.'

Nathaniel followed gratefully. Now that he was up close, he could see that the vicar was a surprisingly well-built man who looked as if he might have been more than a match for Maggot Harris.

'I've seen plenty of fellows like him,' the vicar went on as he led the way through a room at the back of the church filled with tall wooden cupboards. 'I was a soldier before I became a vicar, you know. You get bullies in the army as well. Plenty of decent chaps too, of course. Well, here you are.' He opened a door that led onto the street behind the church. 'Best not to hang about too long,' the vicar advised. 'It won't take him long to work out where you've gone.'

'Thank you,' Nathaniel said again.

'Just try to stay out of trouble,' the vicar advised him.

Nathaniel hesitated. 'Can I ask you something?' he said.

'Certainly. Ask away.'

'If you saw someone who wasn't really there, what would you think?' Nathaniel asked.

The vicar looked bemused. 'Someone who wasn't really there?' he said. 'I'm not sure I follow.'

'A ghost, I mean. Leastways, I suppose that's what it must have been,' Nathaniel told him.

The vicar's countenance darkened. 'Have nothing to do with unquiet spirits,' he told Nathaniel sternly.

'I don't want to have anything to do with them,' Nathaniel replied as he stepped outside into the daylight. 'It's them what's having something to do with me.' He sighed. 'It doesn't matter, anyway. I'm just going to shut my eyes if they come back. Bye then.'

It took him a moment or two to get his bearings. Then he saw the familiar silhouette of the Whitechapel Hospital in the distance and he set off homewards. His flight from Maggot Harris had taken him away from his usual haunts and this was a much more mixed area. There were slums, to be sure, but also some smarter areas with big houses whose inhabitants employed four or five servants. He wondered, as he walked through these streets, what it would be like to live in such a house, not to have to spend your morning carting boxes of fish to earn the price of a loaf of bread, but always to have your breakfast put down on the table for you by a maid. It was almost unimaginable.

The thought of breakfast served on a table spread

with white linen and eaten with the finest silverware reminded him that he had eaten nothing since the previous day, and suddenly a wave of weakness overtook him so that he was forced to stop and lean on the railings outside one of the big houses.

'I'll be all right in a moment,' he told himself. 'Just need to get my strength back.'

But he didn't seem to be getting any stronger at all. In fact, the longer he stood there, the more light-headed he felt.

'I'll just sit down on the pavement for a minute or two,' he told himself as he slid down the railings. There was a buzzing in his head, and he was reminded for some strange reason of the time he had come across a dead cat in the yard outside the William Wilberforce Memorial Hall. Whatever it was that had killed it, the rats had been at it since then and half its stomach had been eaten away. A swarm of flies was buzzing around it and the sound they made was just like the noise he could hear in his head right now.

Nathaniel clutched on to the railings like an animal in a cage while the buzzing in his head grew louder and louder, and the world outside grew darker and darker until the darkness and the buzzing were one and the same thing and he collapsed on the paving stones in a faint.

6. BELOW STAIRS

Lily came up the stairs from the kitchen with a pot of tea, two of Mrs Simpson's fruit scones, a generous pat of yellow butter and a dish of home-made strawberry jam. The scones were still warm and smelled absolutely delicious, and she was thinking to herself that Miss Sophie would surely be tempted to eat a bite this morning, when she looked up and saw Mr Chesterfield standing in the hallway staring at her with an odd expression on his face. She gave a half-curtsy and stepped around him in the hope of getting away as quickly as possible.

But Mr Chesterfield had other ideas. 'Good morning, Lily!' he said with uncharacteristic friendliness.

'Good morning, sir.'

'I see you're bringing Miss Sophie her mid-morning tea.'

'Yes, sir.'

'As a matter of fact I was just on my way upstairs,

myself. Why don't I take the tray and save your legs?' He smiled at her insincerely.

'Just as you please, sir.' She handed over the tray and made her way downstairs again.

'I'll never understand Mr Chesterfield,' she said, as she entered the kitchen. 'Just now he took Miss Sophie's tray from me, saying he wanted to save my legs. But earlier this morning when Miss Pemberton came to call, he flew into a temper and threw her out.'

Miss Pemberton had been a very old friend of Sophie's mother. The two women had grown up together and before the mistress's death, Miss Pemberton had often called at the house, though until this morning Lily could not remember seeing her since the funeral. Lily was fond of Miss Pemberton, for she never failed to ask how Lily was getting on and smile at her as if she really meant her enquiry, unlike some ladies and gentlemen who treated a maid as if she were no more than a piece of furniture.

George, the footman, was sitting at the table cleaning a pair of brass candlesticks with a rag and a bottle of vinegar. He gave her the look he reserved for children and simpletons. 'That's because he blames Miss Pemberton for the will, of course,' he told her.

'What do you mean?' Lily replied, mystified.

'When the mistress died, Mr Chesterfield thought he'd get her money,' George explained, 'but he didn't know she'd made a will a few months earlier leaving all the money in a trust for her daughter when she comes of age. So now he doesn't get a penny unless something happens to Miss Sophie.'

'God forbid!' interposed Mrs Simpson from the other end of the room, where she was standing over an enormous saucepan of chicken stock.

'Naturally he was furious when he found this out,' George continued, 'and he blamed Miss Pemberton on account of the fact that the mistress went to see her not long before she died. He reckoned that it was Miss Pemberton what put her up to it.'

'How do you know all this?' Lily asked.

'I keep me ears open,' George said, looking pleased with himself. 'Besides, I happen to know a chap what delivers documents for Grimes and Cheapstowe. That's the family solicitors,' he added when Lily looked at him blankly. 'He was in the office the day the will was read. He said Mr Chesterfield made a terrible scene. Threatening to contest the will, he was, and everybody in the building could hear him shouting.'

'Never mind you and your friends in high places!' Mrs Simpson said. 'I want to know what's going on outside.' She had forgotten about her stock and was gazing out of the window at the pavement above.

George got up and went to see what she was looking at. 'Just somebody passed out on the flagstones,' he said.

'I reckon he's dead,' Mrs Simpson said. 'I've been watching him for the last five minutes and he hasn't moved a muscle. And I can tell you, the master won't be happy if he finds a young lad passed away on our doorstep.'

'Well, what do you expect us to do about it?' George asked.

'He's got to be moved,' Mrs Simpson replied. 'He can't stay there, blocking up our entrance, that's for sure.'

'Someone will have to go and fetch the Peelers, then,' George said.

'I'm not calling the Peelers until I know he's dead for certain,' Mrs Simpson declared. 'Lily, go and take a look at him.'

Lily looked dismayed. 'Why me?' she demanded. 'Why can't George do it?'

George shook his head firmly. 'It's unlucky for a footman to go near a corpse,' he declared. 'Everyone knows that.'

'First I've heard of it,' Lily told him.

'Well, it's true,' he replied firmly. 'And you don't

want to bring bad luck on the house, do you? Besides, what's your official title?'

'Maid-of-all-Work,' Lily admitted, reluctantly.

'There you are then. A footman's duties is specific whereas yours is general. And enquiring as to the condition of boys what drop dead on the doorstep comes under general duties.' With that, he folded his arms and looked immensely pleased with himself.

'Oh, for goodness sake!' Lily said, turning and marching out of the kitchen.

It wasn't that she cared about going near a dead body. After all, she was the one who had discovered Mrs Chesterfield, stiff and cold in her bed. But it was the principal that mattered – the way she was always lumbered with the dirty jobs and George always got off.

She opened the basement door, stepped outside and climbed up the area steps. The boy was lying slumped against the railings and as she got close to him, she stopped and gasped. He was the one who had saved her from being robbed just a few days earlier. She never forgot a face. Now she felt really miserable. A minute ago he had been just anyone. But suddenly he was someone she knew. What did he say his name was? Nathaniel, that was it.

She bent down to examine him and immediately

felt a surge of relief. He wasn't dead at all. She could see his chest rising and falling as he breathed. He'd probably just fainted. She took hold of his shoulders and gave him a shake.

He mumbled something inaudible. It sounded a bit like, 'The dead are always with us,' but perhaps she had just imagined that. 'Wake up!' she said, shaking him again, more vigorously this time.

His eyelids flickered open and he stared at her in bewilderment. 'Where am I?' he asked.

'You're lying on the pavement outside my master's house,' she told him.

He sat up and looked about him. 'Where's Maggot Harris?' he demanded.

'I don't know any Maggot Harris,' she replied.

Nathaniel frowned and studied her face. Why was she so familiar? Then he remembered. 'Yes you do,' he told her. 'Maggot Harris is the one that tried to rob you.'

'Oh, him!' Lily said. 'He's nowhere to be seen, so you needn't worry. Listen, I should get up if I were you, unless you want to wait there until my master finds you. Then he'll most likely have you arrested as a vagrant.'

Nathaniel looked at her indignantly. 'I'm no vagrant,' he insisted.

'I never said you were,' Lily pointed out. She

thought for a minute. 'Seances, that's your game, isn't it?'

'It's my father's game,' Nathaniel replied. 'I'm just his assistant.' Gingerly, he got to his feet, but he was still very weak and almost immediately his legs began to buckle. He clutched onto the railings for support.

Lily studied him more closely. 'I know what's the matter with you,' she announced. 'You look like you haven't had a decent meal for a fortnight. Proper skeleton you are. Tell you what, come into the kitchen with me. Mrs Simpson's cooking will soon put a bit of life back into you.'

Nathaniel needed no further invitation.

Mrs Simpson and George stood regarding him doubtfully as he followed Lily into the warm glow of the kitchen.

'Here! This is a respectable house,' Mrs Simpson declared. 'It ain't no home for waifs and strays.'

'This is Nathaniel,' Lily replied. 'He's neither a waif nor a stray. He's the boy who saved me from being robbed. You remember? I told you about it.'

'What was he doing on our doorstep, though?' George demanded. 'Come to collect a reward, have you?'

'No, he has not!' Lily replied before Nathaniel could even open his mouth. 'He's collapsed of hunger, that's all. And I think the least we can do is give him a bite to eat.'

There was nothing further George could say. Lily could be just as determined as *he* could, if she wanted. She sat Nathaniel down at the table and looked at Mrs Simpson expectantly.

'All right then,' Mrs Simpson agreed, grudgingly. 'He can have a bit of bread and cheese and there's some of that apple pie left over. But I'm not cooking anything special for him.'

Nathaniel wolfed down the bread and cheese. Only when every crumb was eaten did he look up, to find that everyone was staring at him.

'Blimey!' George said. 'It's like watching a wild animal.'

'He's just hungry, that's all,' Lily said, defensively. Then she put a plate of apple pie in front of him and frowned. 'Eat it more slowly!' she told him, under her breath.

Nathaniel did his best to dispose of the apple pie in a more civilised manner. When it was finished he sighed with pleasure. 'That was the best apple pie I've ever eaten,' he said.

Mrs Simpson positively beamed. 'My late husband, Arthur, God rest his soul, used to say to me, "Mavis, your apple pies are one of the wonders of the modern world,"' she declared. 'He was a man who was very fond of his food,' she added, approvingly.

'Well I reckon that apple pie just about saved my life,' Nathaniel told her.

'Come on,' Lily said, deciding the flattery had gone far enough. 'You can earn your keep by giving me a hand.' She led him into the scullery where a row of boots and shoes were laid out on the floor ready for cleaning and polishing.

'What a lot of shoe leather!' Nathaniel remarked. 'How many people are there living here?'

'Two, apart from the servants of course.'

'Just two? With all of this?'

'It's easy to see you've never been in service,' Lily told him. 'Otherwise you'd know that ladies and gentlemen are forever changing their boots and shoes. Not to mention their hats and coats and gloves and everything else. And they all need to be kept clean. Come on then, let's get started.'

'So what's it like working here?' he asked as he took the laces out of a pair of boots and began washing off the dirt with saddle soap.

'It's a lot of hard work,' Lily told him. 'Not that I mind a bit of hard work really, not if I'm employed in a happy household.'

'I take it this isn't a happy household, then?'

'It used to be a lovely place when the old master

was alive, but he was taken ill and died three years ago. My mistress took her husband's death very bad indeed and it seemed at first as if she would never leave off mourning. But she was too young and pretty to stay a widow for ever.'

'So she married again?'

'Yes, she did. And that was the worst day's work she ever did. I don't know where she met him but I could tell right away he was only after her money. For some reason she couldn't see it, though. Of course he was all charm and compliments when he was courting her. And I suppose she fell for it. Anyway, they were married within six months. And what a change that brought about to our household! Talk about penny-pinching! Every little luxury was cut out. There were no more visits to the zoo or the theatre for my mistress, no more new clothes. Even the housekeeping budget was reduced. And such a foul temper he turned out to have. The first time I heard him raise his voice to my mistress I wanted to march in there and ask him who he thought he was, coming into her house and acting like he owned the place.'

She handed him a pot of blacking and a rag. 'Make sure you can see your face in those boots,' she told him. 'Otherwise he'll be down on me like a ton of bricks.'

'So has your mistress learned to stand up to him yet?' he asked.

Lily shook her head. 'She never did and she never will now, that's for sure. They hadn't been married more than a year when she fell ill. And she went from bad to worse in no time. The doctor said it was smallpox.'

Tears came to Lily's eyes at the thought of her mistress's fate and she turned her head away so that Nathaniel wouldn't see. 'Maybe she's better off now than if she was still alive and married to that brute,' she added when she had recovered herself.

They said no more then until the shoes and boots were finished and Nathaniel decided it was time he was off.

'Call in, if you're passing this way again,' Lily told him.

'Thanks, I might do that.'

He said goodbye to Mrs Simpson who beamed at him from the range where she was stirring an enormous saucepan of soup. But there was no sign of George. Perhaps he had had his nose put out of joint by the presence of another boy in the household.

Lily let him out by the servants' entrance and he climbed the steps up to the pavement, whistling to himself as he walked down the street with a full belly and the two pennies he had earned still unspent in his pocket.

He hadn't gone very far, however, when he saw a familiar figure coming towards him. It was the scar-faced gentleman he had seen talking to Maggot Harris earlier that day. Nathaniel was tempted to turn and run in the opposite direction but a moment's thought told him that Maggot Harris had probably said nothing about him to his companion. So he carried on, trying to look as unconcerned as possible.

Fortunately, the man walked past without giving him a second glance. He walked up to the front door of the house Nathaniel had just left, took out a key and let himself in.

'Well, well, well,' Nathaniel said to himself. 'So that's the master of the house. Well, I don't think much of his choice of friends.'

With that he set off for home, vowing that despite Lily's invitation, he would stay well away from that house in future, even if it meant he never got to sample another piece of Mrs Simpson's apple pie.

7. COPPERPLATE HANDWRITING

There was no sign of his father when Nathaniel got back to the lodgings they shared. But that was not unusual. After one of his drunken binges, Cicero often spent several mornings wandering around London, looking at the sights as though he were someone visiting the city for the very first time. Each afternoon he would come back full of what he had witnessed, describing to Nathaniel the architecture he had seen or the characters he had encountered, before going to bed early and sleeping for at least twelve hours.

One thing that was unusual, however, was the letter that had been slipped under the door of the parlour. Cicero seldom received any correspondence except for occasional demands for money, which he always threw away unopened. Nathaniel picked it up and glanced at it, intending to put it on the table for his father to open when he came back. But there was something about the handwriting that made him stop and look again.

He peered more closely at the elegant, curved lettering. Copperplate, that was the name for it. Where had he seen writing like that before? He racked his brains. Suddenly, with a sadness so profound it almost took his breath away, the answer came to him. It was just like his mother's handwriting.

Nathaniel stood in the middle of the room, the letter still clutched in his hand, and the years melted away. He was sitting on the floor beside his mother, watching as she drew the letters of his name on a piece of slate. Haltingly, he repeated them after her. He could even remember the way she smelled, like warm bread. Tears came to his eyes and he blinked them away.

He turned the letter over and examined the back where the sender's address had been neatly written:

William Monkton
The Beeches
Lee
Kent

It was from his grandfather!

Nathaniel sat down at the table to think. He knew what would happen if he gave the letter to Cicero. It would be read in secret and nothing of its contents would be divulged. Perhaps it would even be torn to pieces or thrown on the fire in anger. And yet there might be something in the letter about his mother. Or even about Nathaniel himself. But no one would ever know because Cicero had made up his mind years ago that there would be no further communication between himself and the Monktons. And what went for Cicero, unfortunately had to go for Nathaniel too.

Was that fair, Nathaniel asked himself? After all, William Monkton was *his* grandfather. Oughtn't he to have some say in the matter? Yes, he decided, he ought. So what was to stop him opening the letter right now and reading what his grandfather had to say? Who would ever know?

He was just about to tear open the envelope when he stopped again. What if there was something in the letter that his father needed to know? Something urgent that had to be communicated. How would he tell Cicero? He could hardly admit that he had opened the letter and read its contents. His father would be so angry that Nathaniel's life would not be worth living.

This needed careful handling. He examined the letter once again. It had been closed with sealing wax. So it would not be an easy matter to open it without destroying the seal and making it clear that the contents had been interfered with. Nathaniel sat at the table for a long time, trying to decide what to do. Finally, he made up his mind to go downstairs and consult Jeremiah.

He was in luck. Jeremiah was at home, sitting by the fire smoking his pipe. He listened carefully to Nathaniel's problem, then shook his head gravely.

'Interfering with a man's private correspondence is a very serious matter,' he said.

'What about interfering between a boy and his grandfather?' Nathaniel replied.

Jeremiah scratched his chin, thoughtfully. 'You have a point, young Nathaniel,' he conceded. 'They do say that blood is thicker than water.'

'Yes they do,' Nathaniel agreed.

'But on the other hand, your father is a man what places great store by his pride. And a man's pride is the only true possession he has in this world.'

'I have my pride, too,' Nathaniel pointed out.

'Of course you do. And quite right too. I'll tell you what we'll do. We'll let the rats decide.'

Nathaniel was about to ask what on earth he meant but Jeremiah raised one hand to stop him. He crossed the room to the wooden cage where the rats were kept, put on a pair of heavy leather gauntlets that lay on the floor nearby, then bent down and opened the door of the cage a fraction of an inch. Immediately the rats began squeaking feverishly. Jeremiah's gloved hand dipped quickly into the cage and emerged seconds later with a single rat, hanging upside down by its tail. Then he closed the cage door again.

'He looks like a lively little blighter,' Jeremiah observed, as he held the wriggling creature up for Nathaniel to examine.

'How exactly is he going to help us?' Nathaniel asked.

'All in good time,' Jeremiah told him. 'See that box over there? If you would be so good as to pick it up and follow me outside, all will be revealed.'

Nathaniel looked in the direction Jeremiah had indicated and saw a closed wooden box about the same size as the rats' cage. Nathaniel picked it up by the leather handle at the top and followed Jeremiah outside into Mrs Bizzantine's back yard.

'Now then,' Jeremiah said. 'You just set that box on the ground.'

Nathaniel did as he was told.

'Here comes the difficult bit, by which I mean persuading our friend to enter the box. You will notice that there is a panel on the side nearest you what can be slid upwards. Kindly oblige me by tilting the box towards me and lifting up the panel just enough for me to slip Mr Rat here inside. Once he's in, bring down the panel again sharpish and set the box on the ground. It's all got to be done nice and smartly, mind, otherwise he'll do an about turn and take a bite out of your finger what you'll remember for the rest of your life.'

Nervously, Nathaniel tilted the box and opened the panel. With a flick of his wrist, Jeremiah flung the rat inside and Nathaniel closed it up. Then he set the box down on the ground once more and waited to see what would happen next.

'This here is my decision maker,' Jeremiah announced proudly, 'designed and constructed by myself. Inside this box is a maze not unlike the great maze at Hampton Court, except on a much smaller scale. There are only two ways out of this maze, one on the left and one on the right, and they are both equally difficult. All we have to do is wait to see what exit our rat emerges from. If he comes out on the right side, we open the envelope; if he comes out on the left, we leave it closed.'

Nathaniel looked at him in astonishment. 'Is this how you make all your decisions?' he asked.

'Only the difficult ones. Now keep your eye on the box. It never takes them very long to find their way out.'

A moment later the rat's head emerged from the hole in the right-hand side of the box. Its nose twitched and it looked to either side. Then it shot out of the box and across the yard, disappearing into a hole under the house.

'There you are,' Jeremiah announced triumphantly. 'The rat has given his verdict.'

Nathaniel eyed the hole in which the rat had taken refuge. He did not imagine Mrs Bizzantine would be particularly pleased to learn that one of her lodgers made a habit of releasing rats in her back yard.

'It's a bargain, you see,' Jeremiah explained as they made their way through the back door into the downstairs hall. 'The rat in question gets his freedom and I get my answer.'

Nathaniel nodded. He opened his mouth to ask how easy Jeremiah thought it would be to open the letter without disturbing the seal, when the front door opened to reveal Cicero. He greeted them with a broad smile.

'Do you know where I have been this morning?' he asked.

'I can't imagine,' Nathaniel replied.

'The Old Bailey. And what an experience it was! Believe me, there is no building in this great city of ours which has such a dismal aspect. Those massive walls bring a chill to the heart of the beholder. Think of what it must be like to be dungeoned away from liberty in that dreary spot.'

'I'd rather not, thank you,' Jeremiah told him.

'I watched the court itself in session and saw the great wheels of justice turn. You should go there. It would be an important lesson.'

As Cicero continued to describe what he had seen, Nathaniel slipped up the stairs ahead of him and placed the letter on the table. Moments later Cicero followed him in. His eye immediately fell on the letter and the smile faded from his face. 'What's this?' he demanded.

'Oh that!' Nathaniel said, off-handedly. 'I found it on the floor this morning. Mrs Bizzantine must have put it under the door.'

Cicero tore it open and examined the contents. His lips curled upwards in a sneer. 'The impudence of that man!' he muttered to himself.

'Anyone I know?' Nathaniel asked.

Cicero gave him a furious glance. 'Mind your own business!' he snapped, stuffing the letter into his jacket pocket.

For the rest of the afternoon he remained in a foul mood, picking things up and banging them down again, cursing loudly whenever Nathaniel got in his way, complaining about the noise or the smells of Mrs Bizzantine's other tenants, objecting to the weather or the traffic in the street; even the air that he breathed seemed to irritate him by its lack of consideration for the state of his lungs.

Finally, Nathaniel decided he'd had enough. He went out of the house and spent the rest of the evening tramping the streets. He passed little shops and great warehouses, breweries belching white smoke into the sky, tanneries filling the air with foul smelling fumes, rooms full of middle-aged women sewing fine clothes for gentlefolk, and factories where scores of young girls dipped matches in vats of sulphur. But he saw none of it. He was lost in thoughts of his mother. If she was still alive, his life would have been completely different. He was certain of that. She had always wanted the best for him, whereas to Cicero he was no more than an unpaid assistant at best, and at worst a source of irritation.

Night had fallen by the time he returned. Cicero was sitting at the table with his head in his hands. He did not ask where Nathaniel had been or how he had occupied himself. He merely grunted in acknowledgement. Tired after a morning spent carrying boxes of fish to and fro and an afternoon spent walking aimlessly through the streets, Nathaniel went straight to bed and was very soon fast asleep.

He woke in the small hours of the night and immediately felt wide awake. Cicero was lying in the other bed, snoring loudly as usual. Nathaniel remembered the letter from his grandfather and sat up in bed. Now was his chance to read it. By the light of the moon he could see Cicero's clothes lying in a heap beside his bed. The letter was most likely still stuffed in his jacket pocket.

Taking care to make as little noise as possible, Nathaniel got out of bed and tiptoed over to the pile of clothes. His eyes never left his father's sleeping form as he slowly bent his knees, picked up the jacket and felt for the pocket. But just as his fingers closed around the letter, Cicero's snoring reached a crescendo and he shuddered in the bed. Nathaniel froze, expecting his father to wake at any moment. Fortunately, Cicero only turned over in the bed and carried on sleeping.

Carefully, Nathaniel drew the letter out of Cicero's pocket. Then he crept over to the window, held it up to the moonlight and began to read.

Dear Sir,

I write to inform you of the death of my wife, Mary. She passed away peacefully last Friday after a long and painful illness. In light of the feelings you expressed when we last spoke, you may wonder why I am troubling you with this news. It is just that at the end of her life, Mary's greatest regret was her separation from her daughter and grandson. 'So many wasted years!' Those were her last words to me.

I see now that she was quite right, and in her absence I realise more clearly than ever what a terrible loss this dreadful quarrel has brought about for all of us. I am conscious that there is only a limited time left to me to make amends and I would dearly love to see my grandson before I too am called to join my wife.

I am writing, therefore, in the hope that some sort of reconciliation can be effected between us. For my part, I am more than ready to admit that I may have been too severe in my criticism of you. I apologise for whatever I said that may have given offence and I beg you to look into your heart and consider whether it is not time to let bygones be bygones.

Yours sincerely,
William Monkton

As Nathaniel reached the end of the letter he felt a great longing to meet his grandfather, to go where he was wanted for once. However, he had not been thinking this very long when he began to notice that the air in the room had become markedly colder.

He shivered and looked up. Beside his bed a pale shape had begun to form – the figure of a woman, its outline blurred and hazy at first but growing clearer all the time. A sense of panic overcame him and he wanted to turn and run but he was rooted to the spot – while the temperature in the room continued to drop further and further, down below zero, where all life threatens to stop. The air around him crackled with frost as the presence beside his bed grew stronger and stronger, coming through from a world where there was no need of warmth to move the blood in the veins, a world that ought to have no contact with ours at all except in one direction – outwards through the gate of death.

But the woman who stood before him, regarding him with the same chilling expression she had worn on the stage of the William Wilberforce Memorial Hall, was defying the rule of nature. She was forcing her way back into the world of the living by the sheer strength of her will, fighting against the great eternal current that wanted to wash her back into death. Nathaniel could sense this. And he knew, also, that he was the reason. She had come back from beyond the grave for him. Nathaniel could not help himself. He gave a cry of terror.

Immediately the woman vanished. At the same time Cicero sat up in bed. 'What in God's name…?' he demanded, staring in confusion at Nathaniel's figure silhouetted against the window. Gradually his eyes adjusted to the darkness and he saw the letter clutched in Nathaniel's hand. With a curse, he sprang out of bed, crossed the room and seized it, at the same time dealing Nathaniel such a blow that he fell to the ground, his ears ringing. 'How dare you read correspondence that is addressed to me!' he cried.

'It's from my grandfather,' Nathaniel said. 'He wants to see me.'

'Then he must continue to want!' Cicero thundered. 'He thinks he's so high and mighty because he happens to be a magistrate. Well, let me tell you something: I may not be as familiar with the law as he is but I am your father and I know my rights.'

With that he flung open the window, bent down and seized Nathaniel, twisting his arm behind his back viciously.

'We'll see who's in charge around here!' Cicero continued, pushing Nathaniel towards the window so that he lost his balance and tumbled forwards. At the same time, Cicero let go of his arm and grabbed him by the legs, up-ending him. In seconds Nathaniel found himself dangling helplessly out of the window with Cicero hanging on to his legs. For the second time that night he thought that his last moment had come.

'Don't kill me!' he screamed, sheer terror racing through his veins.

'By God, I've a good mind to!' Cicero shouted at him. But at last he hauled Nathaniel back inside and flung him down on the floor. 'That's what will happen if I ever catch you going through my things again,' he declared. 'Only next time, I swear on your mother's grave, I will let you fall.'

8. A CONSPIRACY UNMASKED

It was Wednesday night, and as Nathaniel sat inside the door of the William Wilberforce Community Hall collecting pennies from the clients, the thought of the woman in white preyed on his mind. Would she appear on the stage once more? What did she want from him, anyway? If I was dead, I'd stay dead, he thought to himself. I wouldn't go bothering the living by haunting them. It's a cruel thing to do.

'Ain't you got a smile for one of your regular customers?'

It was Mrs Gaunt. Nathaniel did his best to look pleased to see her.

'Busy, tonight,' she said. 'The word's getting round about your dad. If this carries on you'll soon have to find a bigger hall.'

It was true. When Cicero had first started holding

his seances, the hall had been empty. Now there was standing-room only every Wednesday night.

'I do hope your dad has something for me this evening,' she said, giving him a wink before she made her way into the foyer.

While he continued to take money from the long line of customers, Nathaniel watched her mingling with the crowd, sympathising with their grief, ferreting out her little pieces of information and storing them away in her mind. At last everyone was inside, the majority sitting down on the rows of chairs facing the stage, but a small crowd still milling about at the back of the hall, Mrs Gaunt among them.

'My poor Walter,' he heard her telling one elderly woman. 'He never missed a day's work in his life. Much good it did him, though.'

The woman, a tiny little person who wore a wig that had slipped rather comically to one side revealing the pink of her scalp beneath, nodded vigorously. 'My Archie was just the same,' she replied. 'He worked all the hours that God gave. Worked himself into the grave, if you ask me.'

'What business was he in?' Mrs Gaunt asked.

While the two of them were deep in conversation, Nathaniel noticed a sandy-haired gentleman standing nearby who seemed to be listening intently to what they were saying. His face looked familiar and

Nathaniel suspected that this was not the first seance he had attended. But there was something about him that did not seem right. He didn't have the same air of gloom as the other clients. If anything, there was a glitter of excitement in his eyes. Suddenly, he stepped forward and interrupted Mrs Gaunt. 'Why do you ask so many questions, madam?' he demanded, speaking loudly enough for everyone to hear. All over the room heads swivelled in his direction.

Mrs Gaunt looked affronted. 'If you don't mind, sir, this lady and I was just having a private conversation. I don't see what business you have interfering in that.'

'I'll tell you what business I have,' he replied. 'I've come to these seances for four weeks running and every time I've seen you here, asking people questions, and that strikes me as very curious indeed. What's your purpose, that's what I want to know?'

Mrs Gaunt put her hands on her hips, her face a picture of indignation. 'I don't know what you're talking about,' she replied, 'but I would ask you to behave with a little bit of respect and decorum. This lady here has only recently suffered a tragic loss and she doesn't need someone like you causing her aggravation at this difficult time.'

It was an impressive response but the sandy-haired gentleman merely smiled. 'It is not about this lady that I am curious, madam. It is about yourself.'

'Well, you can take your curiosity some place else then,' Mrs Gaunt said, turning her back on him.

The sandy-haired gentleman stood looking at her for a moment longer, then he shrugged and moved away. Nevertheless, Nathaniel could see that a great many members of the audience had overheard this exchange and they were looking at Mrs Gaunt with suspicion. He moved into the hall and began shepherding them to the remaining seats.

'Almost ready to start now, ladies and gentlemen,' he said. 'If you wouldn't mind taking your places.'

It was at this point that Mrs Gaunt normally slipped backstage, but that would have looked much too obvious tonight. So she said something to her companion about feeling too upset to continue, then walked past Nathaniel and out of the main doors. She would have to enter again at the rear. Nathaniel made sure that all the blinds were firmly closed. It wouldn't do for anyone to spot her making her way around the side of the building.

It had been a difficult few moments and though Mrs Gaunt had handled it well enough, she and his father would have to think of a new way of operating. She could hardly turn up again next week and start asking questions in the usual manner. Anyone who had witnessed tonight's altercation would immediately be on their guard. Fortunately, that was not Nathaniel's problem. He made sure that everyone was sitting down in their places. There was just one empty seat at the back of the room, where Mrs Gaunt should have been. Satisfied that everything was in order, he turned down the gas lamps and waited for his father to walk out onto the stage.

Cicero took longer than usual to appear and when he did, Nathaniel thought he looked a little flushed. He knew what that meant. His father had resorted to a drop of gin in order to calm his nerves. It was to be hoped that he had not had too much.

Everything went well enough at first. He made the usual introductory speech, then sat down in the red velvet armchair and sank into his fraudulent trance. A few moments later he was calling for someone called Edwina. A very tall woman with her hair tied back in a severe bun got up, and Nathaniel led her up onto the stage.

'Mother, it's me, Daniel,' Cicero crooned.

The woman's eyes filled with tears.

'I want you to know that I didn't feel a thing, mother. One minute I was walking through the mud, holding my rifle up above my head to keep it dry. Next minute I was here.'

'This is all a fraud!' It was the sandy-haired

gentleman. He had got to his feet and was shouting at Edwina. 'I heard you tell the woman who was asking all the questions that your son was killed in the Crimea. She obviously went and told him afterwards. It's a put-up job!'

Several members of the audience were trying to make him sit down and be quiet and there were shouts of 'Shame on you!', but others were nodding their heads and muttering in agreement. Cicero was sitting in the centre of the stage, staring blankly at the man, and Nathaniel could tell from the expression on his face that he had no idea what to do next. He wondered whether he ought to turn the lights back on and call the whole thing to a halt.

He was just about to do so when he noticed something that made him stop. The empty seat at the back of the hall was empty no longer. A woman dressed in white was seated there and as Nathaniel watched, she turned her back on the stage so that she was facing him directly. It was her!

He could no longer hear the other people in the room; they were entirely forgotten. All that mattered now was the woman who had come from beyond the grave to haunt him yet again. Her eyes were fixed on his and, looking into their depths, he felt he understood the true meaning of hell. It was not a place full of fire and brimstone where devils tormented their victims with pitchforks. Hell was a desire to change something in life when you were no longer living. Hell was an unfinished business that would not let a spirit rest. Hell was a claim that the dead still had upon the living. Hell was the torment that this woman was suffering and Nathaniel was the one with whom she had chosen to share it. There was only one way out of that hell. He had to find out what she wanted.

The woman nodded her head, ever so slightly, as if she understood exactly what he was thinking. Then she raised her arm and beckoned him forwards. He did not want to go. Every fibre of his being screamed at him to resist. And yet he found himself walking slowly forwards.

The nearer he got to the woman, the more he felt as if he might be sick at any moment. This should not be, he told himself. The dead should not have dealings with the living. But the woman continued to beckon and Nathaniel continued to walk forwards.

Finally, he was standing right in front of her and now, at last, she seemed satisfied. She raised her other hand and Nathaniel saw that she held a needle between her finger and thumb and on her lap was a piece of embroidery. As Nathaniel watched, she deliberately drove the needle into the ball of her thumb and took it out again. A bead of blood appeared.

The blood dripped down onto the piece of embroidery.

Suddenly the lights went on in the hall and the woman vanished. The sounds and the sights of the everyday world returned. The room was in uproar. Cicero was standing up on stage raising his arms and appealing for calm.

'The seance is over, ladies and gentlemen,' he said. 'The spirits have withdrawn their co-operation. They will speak to me no more this evening. I must ask that you all leave the hall and go home immediately. I'm sorry there is nothing further I can do tonight.'

Some of the audience stood around the sandy-haired gentleman arguing and it was clear that he had his supporters as well as his critics. But gradually people began to leave the hall in dribs and drabs. A crowd approached Nathaniel demanding their money back. But Nathaniel was too confused and exhausted by his own ordeal to take any notice. He merely stared silently back at them until Cicero got down from the stage and came over.

'There will be no refunds,' he told them firmly. 'The problem was not of my making. If you wish to seek redress, I advise you to speak to our friend over there.' With his thumb he indicated the sandy-haired gentleman. 'However, I must ask you to do so outside. The hall is closing. So if you would kindly make your way outside.' He opened his arms to shepherd them out and reluctantly they began to move in the direction of the exit.

At last they were all gone and only Nathaniel and Cicero remained in the hall. Nathaniel waited for the explosion of anger which must surely come. He felt that he knew exactly what his father would say. Why had he not turned on the lights and called the proceedings to a halt? Why had it been left to a member of the audience? And why had he stood around in a dream afterwards instead of ushering the crowd outside? Briefly, Nathaniel considered walking out into the night and leaving his father to close up the hall by himself, but to do so would only have been to postpone the inevitable. So he sat meekly on a chair in the middle of the hall, like a lamb awaiting the slaughter.

But to his surprise, Cicero did not shout or rage at him. Instead, he sat down on a chair next to him and put his head in his hands. For a long time he remained that way, without speaking. But at last he raised his head and looked at Nathaniel with eyes that were filled with tears. 'What will become of me without Mrs Gaunt?' he whispered. 'How can I learn the secrets of the dead?'

Nathaniel looked back at him and shook his head slowly. He could think of nothing to say that might possibly help.

9. AN ACCIDENT IN THE PARLOUR

There was so much dust in the world, Lily thought to herself as she carefully took down the ornaments from the mantelpiece in the front parlour and wiped each one with a damp cloth. She often wondered where it all came from. If you entered a room when a sunbeam was slanting through the window pane, you could see it falling silently through the air, an endless rain of particles, layer after layer, piling up on every surface like soft grey moss. If it weren't for people like me, wiping it all away, the whole world would be buried in dust, she told herself.

The words the vicar had said at her poor mistress's funeral came into her mind. She could picture him picking up a handful of earth, throwing it on top of the coffin as it was being lowered into the ground and solemnly intoning, 'Earth to earth, ashes to ashes, dust to dust.'

Was that where it all came from, then? Had every speck of dust which now floated aimlessly through the air once been part of someone who lived and breathed, someone who went about their business, laughing at public jokes and weeping at private sorrows?

She wiped the mantel shelf and replaced the ornaments one by one. Then she made her way out into the hall and from there to the back parlour. The two parlours were all one really, but folding doors had been drawn across the middle to make two rooms and each one had its own entrance from the hall. The front parlour was used for receiving guests, but the back parlour was used for nothing at all. At least, not these days. Once upon a time her mistress had sat there in the evenings, practising the piano for hours on end. She played so beautifully, her hands stroking the keyboard as if it was a living thing, drawing such beautiful music from those black and white keys.

Miss Sophie played too, of course, but nothing like so well as her mother. And since Mrs Chesterfield's death she seemed to have given up her music altogether, along with a lot of other things. She was wasting away, poor girl, never leaving the house any more, hardly eating enough to keep a bird alive. Still, at least she had got out of bed and dressed this morning, even if she had done no more than sit in her room all day, listlessly turning the pages of an illustrated book. Yesterday she had spent the whole day lying down, complaining of pains all over her body, until Lily had thought the doctor would have to be summoned. But Miss Sophie had not wanted the doctor. 'I'm just a little off colour,' she had insisted. 'I'm sure to be better tomorrow.'

It was all so horribly reminiscent of the way Mrs Chesterfield's illness had begun. At first she had just seemed a bit lacking in energy, her appetite had diminished and she had lost interest in all her usual pastimes. Then, gradually, she had gone into a decline, spending more and more time in bed until it was clear to everyone in the house that the mistress was dying and there was not a thing that could be done about it. The doctor had come and gone, prescribing strengthening medicines and fortifying tonics. He might as well have poured the whole lot straight down the drain for all the good they had done. The life had slipped away from her mistress as inexorably as the dust continued to fall though the air.

Lily ran her cloth over the dark ebony wood, feeling as if she was paying her respects to her mistress by doing so. On top of the piano was a framed daguerreotype of Miss Sophie which had been taken at a photographer's studio in

Regent Street only twelve months earlier, just before Mrs Chesterfield became ill. Miss Sophie was wearing her very best crinoline dress, her jacket buttoned tightly over her bodice and her bonnet held neatly on her lap. She stared solemnly out of the picture, like a child at Sunday school.

Lily had no idea how the process of photography worked but she had seen a photographer taking a picture out in the street once, when she had gone into town with her mistress. They had crossed over by Westminster Bridge and there he had been with his tripod and black cloth, taking a picture of the River Thames. A crowd had gathered around to watch, as if he was a magician. Well it *was* like magic, as far as Lily was concerned, capturing a person's image forever on a piece of card. But what a pity there was no photograph of her mistress. It would have been nice to be able to pick it up and look at the likeness of Mrs Chesterfield as she had been before she became ill.

Next to the photograph of Miss Sophie was a framed piece of embroidery. It was only half done. Mrs Chesterfield had begun work on it before she became ill, intending to have it completed for Miss Sophie's birthday, but now it would never be finished. After her mother's death Miss Sophie had had it framed just as it was.

Lily picked it up and considered it. There was a border of flowers on a white background. In the centre were the words:

21 September 1861
To a beloved daughter
from her loving mother

But only half the flowers had been stitched. All the same, what was completed was very prettily done. Her mistress had always been good with her needle.

Lily was just about to put the embroidery down on the armchair so that she could dust the top of the piano when she noticed a blood-red stain in one corner of the material. Surely that had not been there before? She would certainly have noticed it.

Even as she stood there, holding the embroidery in her hand, the stain seemed to grow bigger before her eyes, creeping across the picture as though the frame itself was filling up with blood. Lily stared, transfixed for a moment, before screaming at the top of her voice and dropping the embroidery in horror. It fell onto the tiled area in front of the fireplace and the glass shattered.

Lily was still standing there unable to move when Miss Sophie rushed into the room. 'What is it?' she cried. Then her eye fell on the embroidery lying on the floor, its glass front broken into a dozen pieces. 'Oh, Lily!' she exclaimed, bending down to pick it up. 'My mother's embroidery! How could you be so careless?'

Lily shook her head. 'I couldn't help it, miss,' she said. 'There was blood all over it. It was horrible!'

Miss Sophie looked up at her and frowned. 'Blood all over it? Whatever are you talking about?'

'It's the truth, miss,' Lily said. 'It started out as just a little stain in the corner but as I watched it grew bigger and bigger, until the whole picture was covered with it.' She began to sob.

Miss Sophie stared back at her. Then she picked up the embroidery and held it up. 'There isn't any blood on it. Look!'

'There was, though. All over it.'

'You're not making any sense, Lily.'

'I know I'm not, but it's true.'

Before either of them could say another word Mr Chesterfield stepped into the room. His glance took in the broken glass and his expression darkened. 'What is the meaning of this?' he demanded.

Lily sighed. If she could not explain to Miss Sophie, how on earth could she expect Mr Chesterfield to understand? But she had to try. 'I was dusting the piano, sir, and I picked up Mrs Chesterfield's embroidery to move it, when all of a sudden I noticed it was stained with blood.'

Mr Chesterfield stared at her. 'You noticed it was stained with blood?' he repeated, slowly.

'I don't understand it, sir. Because there's no blood on it now. Only it was there, sir, I swear it was, and it gave me such a fright that...'

'That she called me,' Miss Sophie interrupted, 'and I took it from her and dropped it. That was when I screamed. I'm very sorry, father. I'll have it reframed out of my allowance.'

Mr Chesterfield looked from Miss Sophie to Lily and back again. He seemed confused. Finally, he shook his head. 'See to it, then,' he said, turning and walking swiftly out of the room.

Lily watched him go in amazement. It was not like him to let the matter drop so lightly. She had expected him to fly into a rage. Indeed she would not have been surprised to have been given her marching orders. It was just one more confusing twist in an already bewildering morning. She turned back to Miss Sophie who was still holding the embroidery in her hand.

'I'm ever so sorry,' she said.

'It doesn't matter,' Miss Sophie told her.

'You can take the money out of my wages, miss.'

'Don't be silly. I'll pay for it.'

'Thanks ever so much for taking the blame, miss.'

'It's all right. Only, you know you really shouldn't make up stories like that.'

Lily looked at her indignantly. 'It wasn't a story, miss. It was the truth. The whole picture was covered in blood.'

'Then why is there no blood on it now?'

Lily shook her head. 'I don't know, miss.'

Miss Sophie shook her head. 'I'm surprised at you, Lily,' she said. 'I always thought you were such a sensible girl.'

'So did I,' Lily agreed.

'Well, I think you'd better go and get the brush and dustpan and clear up the mess, don't you?'

'Yes, miss.'

'And we'll say no more about the blood or the broken glass.'

'No, miss.'

Downstairs in the kitchen they were even less impressed by Lily's story. 'I honestly thought someone had been murdered,' Mrs Simpson said. 'It gave me quite a turn, really it did.'

'Sounded like a pig being slaughtered to me,' George added.

'It was a vision,' Lily told them.

'Stuff and nonsense!' Mrs Simpson told her. 'Kitchen maids don't have visions. At least not if they want to keep their positions.'

'You know what your trouble is,' George told her. 'You've got an overactive imagination. It's a common thing among girls of your age, I've heard. If you want my advice…'

But Lily didn't wait for his advice. She marched out of the kitchen with the dustpan and brush in her hands. They could say what they liked. She knew what she had seen. It *was* a vision, she was certain of it. The question was: what did it mean?

10. LISTENING AT THE KEYHOLE

The day that Lily broke the glass on the embroidery was Miss Sophie's last real day of health. When Lily came back from taking the embroidery to be reframed that afternoon she found that Miss Sophie had retired to bed with a severe headache. From then on she got steadily worse. She smiled weakly when Lily brought her meals up to her room on a tray, but she hardly touched any of the food and more than once Lily heard her being sick in the bathroom.

The previous night her condition had begun to deteriorate dramatically. Her cheeks, which had been pale and bloodless, now became flushed, and it was clear that she was running a high temperature. Lily was kept busy running up and down the stairs with cold flannels to apply to her forehead but it hardly seemed to make any difference. Miss Sophie went from suffering in silence to incoherent babbling while she tossed and turned upon the bed. Lily had seen this before when Mrs Chesterfield had been ill. Delirium, they called it, and for her old mistress it had marked the beginning of the end.

Doctor Lyndhurst was summoned. He had been the family doctor for years, a great lump of a man who was fond of a pinch of snuff and a glass of brandy. He had done nothing whatsoever to help Mrs Chesterfield when the illness had gripped her. True to form, he only shook his head and said that they must watch Miss Sophie constantly in the hope that her fever might break. Lily could have prescribed that treatment herself and saved his fee.

The fever did not break that night. Instead, it raged unabated all through the hours of darkness like a fire that springs up in a warehouse near the docks. The firefighters point their hoses at the flames and throw on bucket after bucket of water but it vanishes into the inferno without making the slightest difference. So it was with Miss Sophie's fever. As the stars faded from the sky, she writhed and twisted between the sheets, muttering about people or places she had not seen for months or even years. Sometimes her expression would grow wild and she would try to throw off the covers and sit up in bed, protesting bitterly when Lily put her arms around her and, gently but firmly, held her down.

It was an exhausting night and Lily had only managed to snatch a few hours' sleep. Yet at six o'clock she had risen again to carry out all her usual duties – lighting fires, making beds, carrying in Mr Chesterfield's breakfast, clearing it away again afterwards – while continuing to keep an eye on Miss Sophie. She was just running up the stairs for what seemed like the hundredth time that morning when the front doorbell rang. She turned to go down again and answer it but George emerged from the kitchen.

'I'll get it,' he told her. 'You look all in.'

It was a sign of the serious condition the household had been plunged into that even George was making an effort to help. Lily thanked him and continued on her way to Miss Sophie's room. But at the turn of the stairs she stopped when she saw who George was admitting. She could hardly believe her eyes! It was the young man who had tried to steal her purse a fortnight ago! What business could he possibly have in this house? She wondered whether she ought to warn her master that his visitor was a thief, but a moment later Mr Chesterfield himself emerged from his study and greeted his guest with a nod of recognition.

Without another word the two men went into the front parlour together.

Lily waited until George had returned to the servants' quarters. Then she came quickly downstairs and crept along the hallway until she was standing just outside the front parlour. Looking around to make sure that no one was coming, she put her ear to the door and listened.

It was immediately clear that her master was very angry. 'What the devil do you mean by coming to the house?' she heard him say. 'I told you never to show your face here.'

The young man said something in reply but Lily could not make it out.

After that Mr Chesterfield began speaking in a low tone and Lily could hear nothing of what he said. She stayed for a few minutes longer but then, fearing that she might be discovered at any moment, went back upstairs to check on Miss Sophie.

After she had made sure that Miss Sophie was comfortable she considered what she ought to do next. She could reveal the visitor's identity to Mrs Simpson and George, but one of them would be likely to tell the master and Lily was not at all sure how he might take the news. If it was anyone else, she might expect them to summon the Peelers right away. But Mr Chesterfield was different. He might not necessarily take her word against that of one of his acquaintances. But what an acquaintance for a gentleman to possess! Lily shook her head in bewilderment. In the end she decided the best thing was to wait and see.

In the afternoon Miss Sophie became less agitated and Lily had a chance to catch up with some of her work. After the incident with the embroidery, she dreaded returning to the back parlour. But it had to be faced. Mr Chesterfield was very clear that every room in the house had to be thoroughly cleaned and dusted daily. No exceptions were permitted.

It was George who had collected the reframed embroidery and replaced it on the piano. Lily had been too busy looking after Miss Sophie to leave the house. Now she crossed the room and picked it up to see what kind of job the framer had made of it. At first it seemed entirely satisfactory. You could not even tell it had been reframed. But when she looked more closely she saw that where once the text had read…

21 September 1861
To a beloved daughter
from her loving mother

…it had now been changed to:

26 March 1862
In memory of a beloved daughter
from her loving mother

Lily stared at the embroidery in horror. If this was George's idea of a joke, then it wasn't the least bit funny. She marched out of the room, downstairs to the kitchen and accosted him.

'I suppose you think it was funny, changing Mrs Chesterfield's embroidery!' she declared.

George stared at her in bewilderment. Then he shook his head dismissively. 'What are you going on about now?' he said. 'Bloodstains again, is it?'

'You know perfectly well what I'm talking about,' she insisted.

'As it happens, I've no idea,' George told her. 'To tell you the truth, women are a mystery to me, and young girls is ten times worse. Always up in the air about something or other. Hysterical, that's the word. So go on, what is it this time?'

He was so infuriatingly smug! It was more than Lily could bear. She felt something snap inside of her and reaching out with her finger and thumb she took hold of his ear.

'Ow!' George yelled. 'Pack it in! That hurts!'

'Lily, you stop that immediately!' Mrs Simpson called out.

But Lily was not listening. George had made one sarcastic comment too many. Ignoring his protests, and Mrs Simpson's outrage, she dragged him out of the kitchen, up the stairs and into the back parlour. Only when he was standing next to the piano did she release her grip.

George rubbed his ear and grimaced. 'You want locking up!' he told her. 'You've gone completely round the twist. Someone ought to tell Mr Chesterfield.'

'Shut up!' she ordered.

He looked at her in amazement.

She picked up the embroidery and held it out. 'Do you deny that you were responsible for this?' she demanded.

'Course I don't deny it,' he said. 'Someone had to go and fetch it from the picture framer's since you were too busy fussing around Miss Sophie.'

'I'm not talking about fetching it from the picture framer's,' Lily said indignantly. 'I'm talking about this.' She pointed to the text.

'I don't know what you're on about,' George said. 'All I did was pick it up and bring it home. Are you telling me there's something wrong with it, 'cause if there is, it's nothing to do with me.'

'Read it!' Lily ordered.

George shrugged. 'If it makes you happy.' He

took the embroidery from her and read aloud, "21 September 1861. To a beloved daughter, from her loving mother." Satisfied now?'

Lily snatched it back from him and examined the embroidery. Sure enough, the text was exactly as he had read it. 'It was different when I looked before,' she said, falteringly. 'The date was changed and it said, "In memory of a beloved daughter". Now it's gone and changed back.'

George frowned. 'You really have gone barmy,' he said.

'It's the truth!' she insisted.

But George merely shook his head and walked away, muttering darkly to himself.

Lily looked at the embroidery once again but the words were just as he had read them. She put it back in its place on top of the piano. Maybe George was right. Maybe she was going crazy. Or maybe someone was trying to give her a message. But, if so, then what did it mean? She shook her head. Things could not continue like this. It was too much for a poor, uneducated kitchen maid. She needed help.

As she stood there, feeling overwhelmed by events, a name suddenly came into her mind: Cicero Wolfe, medium, clairvoyant, summoner of spirits. Unless she was very much mistaken, the poster advertising his seances was still in her bag.

She would go along, she decided. She would see whether the dead could indeed speak from beyond the grave. And if they did she would ask them what it was they wanted from her.

11. THE ORACLE OF THE EAST END

'Mrs Gaunt, I beg you to reconsider your position,' Cicero said.

Mrs Gaunt was unmoved. She stood in the middle of the room with her hands on her hips and a determined look on her face. 'I am sorry, but that is something I will not do,' she declared. 'Nothing on earth would persuade me to suffer such a degrading and humiliating experience again. Not for all the tea in China, Mr Wolfe. Nor all the pennies in Stepney, neither.'

'The gentleman who proved so objectionable last Wednesday will not be admitted,' Cicero assured her. 'So, you see, you have nothing to fear.'

Mrs Gaunt shook her head. 'It's all very well for you to say that, Mr Wolfe, but my reputation has been besmirched. The finger of suspicion has been pointed in my direction and it will not easily be lifted.

How can I go up to clients and ask them about themselves now? They'll be nudging each other and whispering behind my back. I've lost their confidence. And you don't get that back in a hurry, believe me. What if they was to deliberately tell me things what wasn't true? Have you thought of that?'

Cicero had clearly not thought of that. He struck his head with the palm of his hand like someone who has just received the worst possible news. 'Then what am I to do?' he demanded. 'How will I know what to say?'

'You'll just have to use your wits,' Mrs Gaunt suggested. 'Lead them on, bit by bit, and they'll tell you everything you need to know.'

'But how will I even begin?' Cicero asked. 'What names shall I choose?'

'Oh, for goodness sake, Mr Wolfe!' Mrs Gaunt replied. 'Pull yourself together. Just pick one or two that sound likely. Arthur or Mary or Elizabeth. Someone will stand up, you wait and see.'

'That's easy enough for you to say,' Cicero told her.

'Why don't you just cancel tonight's performance?' Nathaniel asked when Mrs Gaunt had gone. 'You can find a replacement for Mrs Gaunt before next week.'

Cicero gave him a look of irritation. 'In case you have forgotten, this luxurious accommodation is not ours by right,' he replied. 'We are tenants here and the rent is due. Unless you fancy sleeping on the street? No? I didn't think so. Besides, I have a number of outstanding bills which must be paid.'

Nathaniel knew what that meant. When Cicero went on his drinking bouts he had a habit of making wagers with his companions. They would bet on anything: whether the following day would be fine or rainy, whether the next passer-by would be a man or a woman, how many fleabites there were on the landlady's arms. No matter how absurd the subject of the wager, Cicero was prepared to hazard money on it. And his companions were happy to encourage him. Nor were they shy about collecting their winnings when Cicero's luck turned sour. Once or twice in the past Cicero had failed to pay up on time and Nathaniel had found him lying in the street outside their lodging house spitting blood and muttering curses to himself.

'The show must go on!' Cicero declared grandly. But the expression on his face suggested that he did not entirely believe his own rhetoric. He put on his coat and went out of the house without another word.

Usually, he and Nathaniel went to the hall forty-five minutes before the seance was due to start. Nathaniel made sure that the chairs were laid out correctly and Cicero spent the time backstage, preparing himself for his performance. But by half past six there was no sign of his father. Perhaps he had gone straight there, Nathaniel decided. So he set out by himself. But when he arrived at the hall there was still no sign of Cicero, even though the first clients were already beginning to queue up outside.

The doors were always unlocked at half past five by the caretaker. So Nathaniel went inside and began setting out the chairs. At five to seven, Cicero appeared. Despite the fact that he had claimed to be penniless earlier in the afternoon, he had obviously been drinking heavily. No doubt he had found someone prepared to extend his credit.

He walked unsteadily between the two blocks of seating and made his way onto the stage where he stood surveying the empty hall.

'Are you sure you want to go through with this?' Nathaniel asked him.

'And why shouldn't I?' Cicero demanded in his most theatrical manner. 'I am the Sage of Stepney, the Oracle of East London. The hidden desires of my clients are an open book to me.'

'All right,' Nathaniel said, 'you know best. Just try to stand still when you talk.'

'I beg your pardon?' Cicero demanded indignantly.

'You're swaying from side to side.'

'I most certainly am not! How dare you! May

I remind you that your job is to collect the money. And at this very moment there is a queue of clients outside waiting to come inside. So I suggest you get on with it and leave the details of the performance to me.' With that, he staggered backstage.

Nathaniel opened the front doors and sat down at his post behind the table. One of the very first people in the queue was the sandy-haired gentleman who had caused such a commotion the week before. Nathaniel shook his head when the gentleman held out his penny. 'You can't come in,' he said.

'Why not? Frightened I might ask more embarrassing questions?' the man responded.

'You've only come to make trouble,' Nathaniel pointed out.

'I am seeking the truth, no more and no less,' the man insisted.

'Well, you can seek it some place else,' Nathaniel said, 'because you're not coming in and that's final.'

'Come on! Stop holding up the queue!' said a thin woman who was standing directly behind him. Her complaint was repeated by several other voices and reluctantly the sandy-haired gentleman turned away.

'You don't want people like that turning up,' the woman said, as she passed her penny to Nathaniel. 'Creates a bad atmosphere and that upsets the spirits.'

Nathaniel nodded and did his best to smile at her. She was one of the true believers who came every week and always left with a glow of satisfaction, whether or not she received a message from the other side.

One of the last people to come through the door was Lily.

'What are you doing here?' Nathaniel demanded.

'I suppose I can come in like anyone else, if I want,' she said belligerently. 'Or isn't my money good enough?'

Nathaniel pushed her penny back across the table. 'You can come in for free,' he said, lowering his voice so that the others wouldn't hear.

Lily put her penny back in her pocket and disappeared inside. One by one the others filed in after her until the hall was full and it was time for Nathaniel to go backstage and give Cicero his cue.

He found his father sitting on a broken chair, drinking from a silver hip flask.

'They're ready for you,' Nathaniel said.

Cicero nodded, took one last swig from the flask, put it in his pocket and got unsteadily to his feet.

'Are you sure you're going to be all right?' Nathaniel asked.

'Of course I'm going to be all right!' Cicero

replied. 'Just go and dim the lights and stop asking stupid questions.'

As soon as the lights were turned down, the buzz of conversation ceased. All eyes were trained on the stage and at last Cicero stepped out from behind the curtain.

He began well enough, the familiar lines rolling confidently off his tongue and, as usual, the audience gazed back at him, spellbound. The grimaces he made when he sat down in the red velvet armchair were perhaps a little wilder than usual but no one except Nathaniel seemed to notice. There was complete silence in the hall when he asked in a very deep voice, 'Is there anybody in the audience called Penelope?'

The silence continued.

'Are you out there, Penelope?'

Why his father had chosen to begin with such an unlikely name, Nathaniel could not imagine. The hall was probably full of women called Agnes, Charlotte, Hannah, Sarah or Lucy. But not a single Penelope.

'You must not be shy, Penelope,' his father insisted.

The audience shifted in their seats but no one stood up.

'I shall leave you for the moment, Penelope,'

Cicero continued, 'but in time you must summon up the courage to respond.' He slumped back in his seat for a few moments, then sat upright again and began to speak in a thin, high voice. 'Aloysius?' he called.

At the back of the hall, Nathaniel put his head in his hands. Where on earth was his father getting these names from?

'Speak to me, Aloysius.'

But Aloysius had as little to say for himself as Penelope. By now the audience were getting decidedly restless. Cicero tried again. 'Edith, are you there?' he demanded in a voice not unlike his own.

On the left-hand side of the hall a small, shrivelled-looking woman got to her feet, leaning heavily on a stick. With a sigh of relief, Nathaniel went across and led her up to the stage.

'Is that you, Cyril?' she demanded when she was standing beside Cicero.

'Of course it is,' Cicero replied.

'What did you do with the money?' she demanded.

Cicero hesitated. 'The money is safe, Edith,' he assured her.

'Of course it ain't safe!' Edith responded angrily. 'Every penny of our life's savings is gone. I want to know what you spent it on. Was there another woman? Tell me the truth!'

'You should not worry about such things,' Cicero crooned.

'I shouldn't worry?' Edith said incredulously. 'And me about to be turned out of house and home? What kind of an answer is that?'

'I can stay no longer,' Cicero told her, slumping back into his chair. 'I must return to the other side.'

The woman looked extremely dissatisfied. Nathaniel took her by the arm and tried to lead her away but she stood her ground. 'You come right back here this minute, Cyril,' she demanded.

'I have a message for Jemima,' Cicero continued, doing his best to ignore her.

'Never mind Jemima,' Edith insisted, banging her stick on the stage. 'I want to speak to Cyril.'

A very fat woman in the front row stood up. 'My name's Jemima,' she volunteered.

'Jemima, this is your husband speaking,' Cicero continued. But in his eagerness to move on from Cyril he had overreached himself.

'My husband's sitting at home, drunk as a lord,' Jemima said, frowning.

How the situation would have resolved itself can only be guessed for it was at this moment that the woman in white reappeared, standing on the stage behind Cicero, looking out at the audience with those baleful eyes.

There was a piercing scream and then a crash. The woman disappeared and Nathaniel looked around to see that several members of the audience had got to their feet. He heard someone say, 'Give her air,' and gradually it dawned on him that somebody had fainted. He left Edith where she was standing, got down from the stage and turned on the lights. A number of people were bending over a figure who was lying prostrate on the floor.

'Could everybody please stand back,' said an authoritative voice.

Nathaniel looked towards the speaker and saw with surprise that it was the sandy-haired gentleman. He must have sneaked into the hall after Nathaniel had gone to give Cicero his cue.

Reluctantly, the crowd began to move away from the figure on the floor and now Nathaniel could see that it was Lily. She was sitting up and looking around her in bewilderment.

'I'm afraid tonight's seance is over,' Nathaniel announced.

There were angry mutterings from the crowd. 'That's two weeks running!' somebody said.

'We want our money back!' someone else called.

Nathaniel glanced towards the stage where Cicero still sat as if stunned. 'If you would kindly make an orderly queue, I will be happy to refund your entrance fee,' Nathaniel announced.

Still muttering unhappily, the audience began lining up next to the table beside the door. Nathaniel went backstage and collected the small leather bag in which the takings were always stored. On the way out he passed Cicero.

'What do you think you're doing?' Cicero hissed.

'Making the best of a bad job,' Nathaniel told him.

'You can't give them their money back,' Cicero protested, but there was no authority in his voice and he looked utterly deflated.

'You didn't deliver the goods!' Nathaniel said. 'What else do you expect me to do?' Then he marched back into the hall.

By the time he had finished giving the customers their money back, Lily was sitting on a chair, the colour restored to her cheeks. 'I saw her, standing up on the stage as large as life,' she was telling the sandy-haired gentleman.

'You're quite certain it was her?' the gentleman asked.

'I ought to know my own mistress,' Lily told him.

'Oi! You weren't allowed in,' Nathaniel said, going over to join them.

The gentleman smiled apologetically. 'I'm afraid my job often requires me to inveigle my way into places I'm not really allowed to enter,' he said.

'Oh does it?' Nathaniel replied. 'And what job would that be, then?'

The sandy-haired gentleman held out his hand. 'Mortimer Pinkus, gentleman of letters, observer of the human condition,' he said.

Nathaniel looked at the outstretched hand but kept his own firmly at his side. 'What's that supposed to mean?' he demanded.

'I write for the newspapers,' Mr Pinkus explained. He added that he was currently conducting an investigation into psychical phenomena.

'I beg your pardon?' Lily said.

'Psychical phenomena,' Mr Pinkus repeated. 'Strange occurrences, unexplained happenings, ghostly manifestations. Anything of that sort.'

'Well, I hope you don't think you're putting me in one of your newspapers,' Lily told him. ''Cause I won't stand for it. And that's a fact.'

'My investigation is still in its infancy,' Mr Pinkus reassured her. 'Nevertheless, I would be interested to hear of any further appearances by the woman in white.' He put his hand in his pocket, took out two visiting cards and handed one each to Lily and Nathaniel.

After he'd gone, Lily helped Nathaniel put away the chairs. As they worked, she described everything that had happened to her in the last few days.

'George and Mrs Simpson won't listen to me,' she told him. 'They think it's just my nerves. I was even beginning to come to the conclusion they might be right until I saw my late mistress standing up on the stage staring out at me. You believe me, don't you?'

Nathaniel nodded. 'Course I believe you. I saw her too, And it's not the first time either.' He told her about Mrs Chesterfield's appearances in his bedroom.

'What do you think she wants?' Lily asked.

'I thought you might know the answer to that,' Nathaniel replied. 'She was your mistress, after all.'

Lily shook her head. 'All I know is that the embroidery said Miss Sophie was going to die in five days' time. I thought your father might be able to tell me what I ought to do.'

Nathaniel looked towards the stage where Cicero, still seated in the red velvet armchair, was now snoring loudly. 'Not much chance of that,' he told her. 'My father's not in a position to tell anyone what to do just now.'

'What are you going to do with him?' Lily asked.

'Well, I shall have to get him home somehow.'

'Do you need a hand getting him upright?'

'Yes, please.'

They went up onto the stage, each took one of Cicero's arms, and at the count of three pulled him to his feet. He muttered something in protest but did not open his eyes.

'How on earth are you going to get him home?' Lily asked.

'Oh, I'll manage somehow,' Nathaniel said.

'I'll come with you, if you like,' Lily said.

'You don't have to do that.'

'I don't mind,' Lily told him. 'I'd just as soon have a bit of company for a little longer, if it's all the same to you.'

'Thanks very much then,' Nathaniel said.

Somehow they got Cicero down off the stage and out of the hall. Then, one on each side, they half led, half dragged him along the street.

It was a mild enough night and the moon shone brightly from behind a gap in the clouds as they made their way slowly back to Stepney. For the most part, Cicero went peacefully enough. Once or twice he stopped and struggled with them, complaining angrily that he was being treated abominably and threatening to summon the Peelers, but his protests soon ran out of steam.

At last they reached Mrs Bizzantine's house where Jeremiah stood outside, leaning on the gatepost and smoking his pipe.

'You remember Lily,' Nathaniel reminded him, as they eased Cicero onto the doorstep where he collapsed in a heap. 'She's the girl Maggot Harris tried to rob.'

'I'm very pleased to see you again,' Jeremiah told her. 'Speaking of the devil,' he went on, 'I've just seen Maggot Harris in a bar in Whitechapel. He didn't see me because he was too busy flashing his money around, buying drinks for his cronies. He seemed to have an awful lot of cash and I heard him say that there was more where that came from.'

'I saw him earlier this afternoon,' Lily told them. She described Maggot's appearance at the Chesterfields' earlier in the day and the way Mr Chesterfield had reacted.

'If you ask me, that Mr Chesterfield is not a man to be trusted,' Nathaniel declared.

'But what does it all mean? That's what I want to know,' Lily demanded.

'I couldn't say,' Nathaniel replied. He looked at Jeremiah, but the tosher merely contented himself with blowing a large smoke ring into the air.

Just then the bells of St Agnes the Martyr struck nine o'clock. Lily looked alarmed. 'I shall have to be getting home, else I'll be in no end of trouble,' she said.

'Do you want me to walk back with you?' Nathaniel said.

Lily shook her head. 'I'll be all right, now,' she told him. 'All I needed was a spot of fresh air.'

'I'll tell you what,' Nathaniel suggested. 'Why don't we meet tomorrow to talk about things further. I mean, we can't just leave the situation as it is, can we?'

'All right then,' Lily agreed. 'It'll have to be after six, though. I can't get free before then.'

'Shall I come round to the house?' Nathaniel said.

'No, I'll come round here.' She nodded to Jeremiah. 'Nice meeting you again.'

Jeremiah bowed. 'The pleasure is all mine,' he said, gravely.

Lily grinned back at him. 'Till tomorrow, then,' she said to Nathaniel.

'Till tomorrow,' he agreed. He watched as she walked away and it occurred to him that there was something about her he could trust. For the first time in as long as he could remember, he felt like there was someone else on his side.

Right now, however, there was still the problem of his father to be dealt with. He turned to Jeremiah. 'You couldn't give me a hand putting him to bed, could you?' he asked.

Jeremiah knocked out the contents of his pipe and slipped it into his pocket. 'Come on then me old china,' he said, slipping his arms under Cicero's and raising him to his feet.

Cicero opened his eyes wide. 'Unhand me, you ruffian!' he protested. 'I am the Oracle of the East End!'

'Course you are,' Jeremiah assured him. 'Nobody doubts it. But you know what? Even oracles has to go to bed sometimes.'

12. THE LAYER-OUT

Nathaniel got up early the next morning and spent the day in Billingsgate working for One-Eyed Harry. By the time he got home in the late afternoon he was bone tired. What he wanted to do most of all was stand under the pump in Mrs Bizzantine's yard and wash away the stink of fish. But Mrs Bizzantine had other ideas. She pounced on him as soon as he went through the front door.

She was a small, stout woman with a barrel-chest and muscular forearms. She stood squarely in front of Nathaniel, blocking the hallway, her arms crossed and a belligerent expression on her face. 'Your dad owes me six weeks' rent!' she informed him.

Six weeks! That was more than Nathaniel had expected. 'I've no doubt he intends to pay you,' he assured her.

'What he intends is of no interest to me whatsoever,' Mrs Bizzantine replied. 'It's what he does that I'm concerned with. Where's he been all day?'

Nathaniel shrugged. 'I couldn't say.'

'I'll tell you where he's been then, since you're so unfamiliar with his movements,' Mrs Bizzantine went on. 'Hiding. That's where. Well, it won't do him no good, let me tell you. If I don't get my rent sharpish, he's out on his ear. And you along with him.'

'I'll be sure to pass the message on,' Nathaniel told her.

'You do that,' Mrs Bizzantine said. 'And you can tell him something else while you're at it. There was a couple of very unpleasant characters round here earlier on looking for him. I could see right away what kind they were. Thugs and 'ooligans, that's all. They wouldn't say what they wanted but you wouldn't need to be a fortune teller to work it out. Money, that's my guess. Well, you just remind him that I'm first in the queue. He can settle his other debts when he's paid the rent. Otherwise it's cobblestones for pillows. Got it?'

Nathaniel nodded.

'Right then.' She stepped aside to allow him past.

Cicero did not show his face for the rest of the afternoon so there was no opportunity for Nathaniel to pass on Mrs Bizzantine's warning. At half past six she knocked on the door of their lodgings to inform him that he had a visitor. He went downstairs and found Lily standing on the front doorstep.

'How are things with you?' he asked her.

'Terrible,' she told him. 'Miss Sophie keeps being sick all the time. She can't keep any food down at all now. It looks very much like the prediction on that embroidery is going to come true. Fortunately, Mr Chesterfield has hired a nurse to sit with her, though it's not before time. Otherwise I'd never have been able to get out of the house.'

'Have you had any more thoughts about what Mrs Chesterfield might want us to do?' Nathaniel asked her.

She shook her head. 'Not really. But I did have one suggestion.'

'Which was?'

'I thought we ought to have a word with Maggot Harris. I've got a feeling there's something wicked going on and he knows all about it.''

Nathaniel looked at her as if she had just sprouted another head. 'Are you completely mad?' he said. 'Maggot Harris would like to cut me into little pieces and feed me to the pigeons.'

'We could ask Jeremiah to come with us,' Lily suggested. 'He's not afraid of Mr Harris.'

'I suppose so,' Nathaniel agreed, without much enthusiasm.

At that moment Jeremiah himself came walking

down the street towards them, carrying a crate of rats in each hand. He looked pleased to see them.

'Do you know where these rats came from?' he asked.

'The sewers of course,' Nathaniel said.

'Ah, but whereabouts in the sewers, that's the question. I'll tell you where,' he continued when neither of them offered a suggestion. 'Mayfair. Where the toffs live. Believe me, where the houses is the fanciest, the rats is the roughest. Look at the size of them. This lot is worth another ha'penny a rat.' He beamed down delightedly at his specimens.

'We were wondering if we might ask you a favour,' Lily began.

'For a young lady such as yourself and a friend of Nathaniel's here, I'd be only too happy to oblige,' Jeremiah assured her. 'You just tell me what you want me to do.'

'Could you come along with us to see Maggot Harris?' Lily asked.

Jeremiah's face fell. 'Ah, now, that's a different matter,' he said. 'It's not that I'm unwilling to help, but there's a small complication.'

'Which is?' Nathaniel asked.

'Maggot Harris was found in the sewers this morning.'

'You mean he's dead?' Lily asked.

'Very much so, I'm afraid,' Jeremiah said. 'I spoke to the tosher what found him myself. He said our friends here' – he nodded towards the rats – 'had already been to work on him. They ain't particular as to how they find their food or how they leave it neither, if you take my meaning.'

They did take his meaning and for a little while no one said any more as they imagined the grisly fate that had befallen Maggot Harris.

'But what was he doing in the sewers in the first place?' Nathaniel asked at last.

'Now that's an interesting question,' Jeremiah replied. 'The Peelers reckon that someone must have left a cover off a drain, and our friend Mr Harris stumbled in during the hours of darkness, banged his head and knocked himself unconscious.'

'So the rats must have eaten him alive?' Nathaniel said in horror.

'Well, perhaps,' Jeremiah agreed. 'Except that the tosher what found him said to me that it looked more like someone had polished him off first then dragged him down there. He said the lump on his head was too big to be got by falling down a hole. But the Peelers didn't want to know when he pointed it out to them. I suppose they've got enough to do without enquiring into the last hours of someone like Maggot Harris. But I'll tell you something that strikes me as odd. I heard that his body's been removed for burial by a proper undertaker and all the bills has been taken care of. Apparently a friend of the deceased has stumped up the cash.'

'Maggot Harris didn't have any friends,' Nathaniel pointed out.

'Exactly,' Jeremiah replied.

Lily sighed. 'Well, we've lost our chance of speaking to him, anyway,' she said, despondently.

'You could try having a word with the undertaker,' Jeremiah suggested.

'Of course!' Lily said. 'Do you know his name and address?'

'Nicodemus Bulstrode, Whitechapel Road,' Jeremiah told her. 'And he don't come cheap, neither, I can tell you. All his clients is very well-heeled. So whoever Maggot's friend is, he's not short of a bob or two.'

Nicodemus Bulstrode's funeral parlour was decorated with purple drapes, held in place by gold tassels. Samples of coffin woods, coffin handles and nameplates were mounted on the wall. Swathes of lining material were displayed in a glass case beneath the counter, and headstones carved in a variety of different lettering leaned against the wall.

'I never thought there was so much to dying,' Nathaniel said, as they walked in and gazed around.

Nicodemus Bulstrode himself was in conversation with an elderly dark-haired woman who stared back at him as if fascinated by every word he had to say. Her dark eyes seemed to glitter in the gaslight and from time to time she reached up a hand to touch an enormous black mole in the centre of her forehead. Mr Bulstrode wrote down something on a piece of paper and handed it to her. Then he wished her good evening and turned his attention to Lily and Nathaniel.

He was a thin man with a poker face, very large eyebrows and hair that was plastered to his scalp with oil. He smelled of candles and incense and something else that Nathaniel could not place, but that could have been the smell of death itself. His welcoming smile rapidly died away when he learned that they had only come for information and not to arrange a funeral. He listened in silence, observing them over the top of half-moon glasses and looking as if he suspected Nathaniel might leave dirty marks on the counter. Finally, he shook his head.

'I'm afraid I cannot be of any help to you,' he told them. 'The body of Mr Harris was certainly received into these premises this morning but I am quite unable to give any information about the circumstances of the death. Furthermore, the financial arrangements for the burial are a confidential matter between myself and the party involved. Now if there is nothing else I can do for you, I must be getting back to business.'

He could not be persuaded to change his mind, but as Nathaniel and Lily reluctantly made their way outside they were approached by the woman with the mole in the middle of her forehead. She had been hanging around just outside the doorway, apparently inspecting some tombstones. Nathaniel suspected she had really been eavesdropping on their conversation and it was soon clear that his suspicion was justified.

'Begging your pardon, young sir and madam,' she began, 'but I couldn't help overhearing your questions to Mr Bulstrode. And I thinks to myself, those two is wasting their time good and proper, on account of the fact that Mr Bulstrode is a very discreet man, you see, and confidentiality is his watchword. His lips are as tightly sealed as a coffin lid, you might say. But of course, confidentiality can be carried too far. Mr Bulstrode don't always see that but you and I know different.'

'And you are?' Nathaniel asked.

'The young gentleman is quite right!' the woman replied, as if she was addressing some unseen third party. 'Those who wish to do business should first introduce themselves. My name is Mrs Marble – cleaner, preparer and layer out of corpses.'

'What exactly were you saying just now about doing business?' Lily asked.

Mrs Marble nodded her head enthusiastically and her eyes seemed to glitter even more than they had in the shop. 'The young lady likes to get to the point,' she observed. 'Which is only natural. Time waits for no one, as Mr Bulstrode's clients will testify. Perhaps if we was to retire to somewhere private, I might be able to put your minds at rest.'

'Where do you suggest?' asked Lily.

Mrs Marble's eyes positively danced. 'I happen to know of a very convenient premises nearby where we can discuss the matter further. If the young lady and gentleman would care to accompany me.'

The convenient premises turned out to be nothing more or less than a gin palace. Lily was horrified at the prospect of stepping inside. 'If I'm seen by anyone who knows me, I might as well go straight back home and hand in my notice,' she objected.

But Nathaniel was more philosophical, having often had to look for his father in similar places. 'If you do happen to meet anyone you know in there, they'll most likely be as keen to keep quiet about it as you will,' he pointed out.

The interior of the building was brightly lit, noisy,

and immensely crowded. Every class and rank of society seemed to be represented among its customers. Gentlemen sat smoking cigars and discussing business, red-faced labourers laughed and swore and thumped each other on the back, bent old washerwomen huddled round tables gossiping, sporting men placed wagers on greyhounds, and mothers dipped their fingers in gin for their babies to suck.

Mrs Marble found an empty table in an alcove and they sat down. Immediately a heavily made-up young woman came over and asked what they wanted. Mrs Marble looked expectantly at Nathaniel and Lily. With dismay, Nathaniel understood that she was waiting for them to order her a drink. 'I've only got a penny,' he said.

Lily sighed. Fortunately, before leaving the house she had plundered the tin box containing her life savings, which she kept under her bed. Though it was Maggot Harris she had expected to be bribing with alcohol. 'A glass of gin for our friend,' she told the barmaid.

'Nothing for yourselves?'

Lily and Nathaniel shook their heads.

Mrs Marble beamed. 'Much obliged, I'm sure,' she said.

'So what do you know about Maggot Harris?' Lily

asked, getting down to business as soon as the barmaid had left them.

'I know that he was in a shocking state when they brought him in,' she replied. 'It looked to me like someone had dealt him a terrible blow to the back of the head. Made a proper mess of his skull, I can tell you. Of course I know the Peelers put it about that he fell down the hole and knocked hisself out, but I can't see it. No, I reckon he got on the wrong side of someone with a nasty temper. Are you relatives, by any chance?'

Lily and Nathaniel shook their heads.

'Well, he must have been very well thought of by someone,' Mrs Marble continued. 'At least, the gentleman what is paying for the funeral told Mr Bulstrode not to worry about the expense. "Money is no object, Mr Bulstrode," he said. "Just spend what you need to and send the bill to me." Now I call that very handsome.'

'Do you happen to know the gentleman's name?' Nathaniel asked.

Before Mrs Marble could reply the barmaid came back with a glass of gin on a silver tray. The glitter returned to Mrs Marble's eyes as she took the glass and sipped its contents with surprising delicacy.

'Now that's what I call a lovely drop of gin. Dry and smooth. Not like the muck they give you in some places. This is the proper ointment.'

'The man who is paying for the funeral,' Lily reminded her. 'Do you happen to know his name?'

Mrs Marble frowned. 'The only trouble is that one glass of gin is never enough,' she said. 'It gets you in the mood, see, but it doesn't satisfy. Whereas two glasses lubricates the memory.'

Lily shook her head. 'We need more information first.'

Mrs Marble looked unhappy.

'I promise I'll buy you another drink,' Lily assured her. 'But only when you've told us something we don't already know.'

'The young lady drives a hard bargain,' Mrs Marble grumbled.

'But I keep my promises.'

Mrs Marble nodded. 'Very well then, let me see. I couldn't tell you the name of the gentleman what came to see Mr Bulstrode but I can tell you this much: he's got a nasty scar on his cheek what mars his features somewhat. Otherwise he'd be a good-looking man.'

'This scar,' Lily said. 'Does it go from here to here?' She drew a line with a finger on her own face.

Mrs Marble nodded. 'You've got him,' she said.

'Did he suggest any reason why he was footing the bill?' Nathaniel asked.

'Only that he was a dear friend of the deceased.'

'And you're sure that Maggot Harris was murdered?'

'Well, now, I wouldn't go so far as to say I was sure. I'm only telling you what I saw with my own eyes, which was that the back of that young man's head was a terrible mess.'

She finished her gin, put the glass down firmly on the table and looked at them expectantly.

'That's all you've got to tell us?' Lily asked, disappointed.

'There was one other thing.'

'Yes?'

'The young man had nothing in his pockets except a receipt from the chemist's shop for six pennyworth of arsenic. He must have had rats to kill, I reckon. That's what they normally use arsenic for, I'm told. But as it turned out, the rats got him first. Chewed one of his ears right off.'

Lily made a face. 'That's horrible!' she said.

Mrs Marble shrugged. 'Poetic justice if you ask me. Now then, how about my second glass of gin?'

They left her in the gin palace eking out her second drink for as long as she could. Afterwards, they walked along the street together, trying to make sense out of what they had just heard.

'Let's consider the facts,' Nathaniel began. 'We

know that some sort of dealings were taking place between Mr Chesterfield and Maggot Harris. And whatever they were up to, it was something your master didn't want anyone to know about. That's why he was so angry about Maggot turning up at the house.'

'We also know that after visiting Mr Chesterfield, Maggot seemed to have come into money,' Lily went on.

'Right,' Nathaniel agreed. 'But then shortly after that he was unexpectedly killed and, despite what the Peelers have said, the manner of his death suggests he was murdered.'

'Of course, he could just have been robbed,' Lily observed. 'Someone might have seen him flashing his money about, waited till he was by himself, knocked him over the head and taken the cash. It's the most likely explanation,' she added.

They stopped at a corner beneath a pawnbroker's sign. A cab horse stood by the kerb, munching steadily from its nosebag and steaming slightly in the cold evening air. This was where they went separate ways.

'Maybe it was just a simple robbery,' Nathaniel said. 'But that doesn't explain everything. Like him turning up at your house unexpectedly, and the receipt in his pocket for arsenic. I suppose he might have just wanted to kill some rats, like Mrs Marble suggested, but then why should your master be prepared to shell out for the funeral of a notorious villain? And why should he want to keep his generosity quiet? There's something about this whole thing that stinks like a dead donkey.' He shook his head. 'Perhaps we should meet up again tomorrow and talk about it some more? Can you get away from the house?'

But Lily was no longer listening. She had turned as white as a sheet. 'I've just had a terrible thought,' she told him.

'What?'

'Arsenic can be used to poison people, as well as rats.'

'You think Maggot Harris was planning to poison someone?'

Lily shook her head. 'I don't know,' she said. 'It's just that I suddenly remembered something George said. He told me that Mr Chesterfield won't get a penny of my poor mistress's money unless something happens to Miss Sophie.'

Nathaniel frowned. 'I don't quite follow,' he said.

'I was taking her mid-morning tea up to her room the other day and he suddenly appeared and took the tray from me,' Lily went on. 'Said he wanted to save my legs. I thought at the time, what's he up to? He's never showed any interest in saving me work before.'

The meaning of her words slowly began to dawn on Nathaniel. 'You think he's poisoning Miss Sophie?'

'I think it's possible,' Lily said. 'He could have got Maggot Harris to go to the apothecary and fetch the poison on his behalf, so that no one would make the connection between him and the arsenic, but then for some reason Maggot turned up at the house in broad daylight.'

'Knowing Maggot, he was probably looking for money,' Nathaniel interjected.

Lily nodded. 'Anyway, Mr Chesterfield might have got uneasy when Maggot Harris started walking in the front door and decided it was time to make away with him.'

'So he was the one who hit him over the back of the head and dumped his body in the sewer. And that's why he's paying the funeral expenses – so that the whole thing can be got out of the way with as little fuss as possible,' Nathaniel suggested.

'Of course, we might just be putting two and two together and making five,' Lily went on.

'We might,' Nathaniel agreed. 'But it fits the facts. Here! I've just thought of something else.'

'What?'

'If he's trying to poison Miss Sophie, maybe he poisoned his wife, as well.'

Lily nodded her head. 'The question is, what are we going to do about it?' she said.

'We'll have to tell the Peelers,' Nathaniel said.

'But do you think they'll listen to us?' Lily asked.

'I don't know, but I think we have to try.'

Neither Nathaniel nor Lily had ever been inside a police station before. They were both very nervous when they went through the doors of the headquarters of Stepney Constabulary and were confronted by a red-faced sergeant with a handlebar moustache. 'And what can I do for you?' he enquired.

'We've come to prevent my mistress being poisoned,' Lily told him.

'And to report a murder,' Nathaniel added.

The sergeant raised his eyebrows. 'Anything else?' he asked.

'Well, there might have been two murders, actually,' Lily said.

'Two murders? Right.' The sergeant opened his notebook, took a pencil out of his breast pocket and licked the end of it. 'You'd better begin by telling me your names,' he said.

It wasn't an easy story to tell, and as Nathaniel and Lily described the ghostly appearances by Mrs Chesterfield, it was clear that the sergeant was becoming less and less sympathetic. He put his pencil down on the table and scratched his head. When they got to the bloodstains and mysterious changes to the wording of the embroidery he put up his hand to stop them.

'All right, all right, I think I've heard enough,' he said. 'This is a police station, not a music hall.'

'You don't believe us?' Lily asked.

'Look, miss,' the sergeant said, 'it's not that I don't believe you. You seem like a decent enough girl and I'm sure you mean well. But you didn't ought to go mixing with the likes of him and his father.' He jerked a finger in Nathaniel's direction.

'What's that supposed to mean?' Nathaniel demanded.

'Swindling honest people out of their money, that's what it is,' the sergeant went on. 'If I had my way, it would be against the law. But unfortunately it ain't. Yet. What I suggest you do is go back home, get on with your work and forget the whole thing. And as for you.' He frowned down upon Nathaniel. 'Just clear off out of here before I think of something to arrest you for.'

'Well, that worked well,' Nathaniel said when they were out on the street once more.

'I'm sorry,' Lily said. 'He shouldn't have said those things to you.'

'It wasn't your fault,' Nathaniel pointed out.

'Besides, most of what he said is true. My father is a swindler and I've been assisting him for years, so I reckon that makes me a swindler, too.'

Lily shook her head. 'We all do what we have to in order to survive,' she told him. 'Anyway, I must go back home now before Mr Chesterfield starts asking what's happened to me. Let's meet up again at the same time tomorrow when we've had a chance to think things over.'

Rather dejectedly, they shook hands and Nathaniel watched as Lily hurried off back to the big house where Mr Chesterfield lurked like a spider in the centre of a web. Then he turned and made his way back towards his lodgings, stopping only to buy himself one of Mrs Jolly's meat pies on the way.

13. CHISELLING CHARLIE

As soon as he turned into his street, however, he knew that something was up. A crowd had gathered around Mrs Bizzantine's house, and as he drew nearer he saw that Cicero was leaning out of the window. He was red in the face, clearly extremely drunk and yelling curses at a small, neatly dressed man wearing spectacles who was standing on the pavement outside the house looking up at him.

At last Cicero seemed to run out of energy and his tirade of abuse came to a halt.

The neatly dressed man looked quite unabashed. 'It will not do, Mr Wolfe,' he called back. 'It will not do, at all. I must insist that you come downstairs and open the door immediately.'

Cicero's head disappeared inside the window and for a moment Nathaniel thought he must have decided to comply with his visitor's request. But a moment later, much to the delight of the crowd, who hooted and cheered with amusement, a plate came flying down from the window, clearly aimed at the little man's head. It was closely followed by a chamber pot.

The little man shook his head and retreated but as he did so he called out, 'You have not heard the last of this, Mr Wolfe!'

The crowd continued to stand around for a little while, waiting to see what would happen next. But at last they came to the conclusion that the evening's entertainment was at an end and melted away into the doorways and alleys from which they had emerged. Only Jeremiah was left standing on the front doorstep, looking very solemn.

'Who was the little man with the big opinion of himself?' Nathaniel asked.

'A chiselling charlie,' Jeremiah told him.

Nathaniel's heart sank. A chiselling charlie was a bailiff, empowered by the courts to recover debts.

'It's a good job Mrs Bizzantine wasn't here to witness this,' Jeremiah went on. 'She's gone to see her sister in Cripplegate. Mind you, I've no doubt she'll get to hear about it in time. She won't stand for it, you know. Between them they'll have your father in the lock-up quicker than a rat down a drainpipe.'

'What am I going to do with him?' Nathaniel asked.

Jeremiah shook his head. 'There ain't nothing you can do with him,' he said. 'Your father's a man what believes in digging himself a hole and then lying down in it. And there ain't no man or woman alive what's going to shift him out of it, unless he makes up his own mind to move.'

'I'll talk to him about it,' Nathaniel said. 'I'll make him listen.'

'I hope so,' Jeremiah said. 'Because otherwise he's going to hell in a handcart. And you can tell him I said that.'

But by the time Nathaniel had let himself into the lodgings Cicero was lying on the bed snoring loudly, the empty hip flask still clutched in his hand. No amount of shaking could wake him. Nathaniel sighed. There was no money to pay debts yet there always seemed to be enough money for gin. Jeremiah was right. His father was on the road to ruin and there seemed to be absolutely nothing that he could do to prevent it.

Nathaniel sat by himself, eating his meat pie and going over the events of the day in his mind while outside the sky gradually darkened and, one by one, the stars came out. At last, when his brain was too tired to think any more, he retired to bed.

He woke in the middle of the night, certain that he had heard his name being called. He was immediately aware of how cold the room had become, so he was not surprised upon opening his eyes to find the figure of Mrs Chesterfield standing in the corner of the room, staring at him. The fear he had felt the first time he saw her had grown less as he had become accustomed to her visits. But her presence still created a sense of panic deep inside him, as if the ground beneath him could give way at any moment and he could find himself sucked down into the very depths of hell.

'I don't know what you want from me,' he told her. 'We went to the Peelers but they laughed in our faces. What else can we do? I can't tackle Mr Chesterfield by myself. You'll have to find someone else.'

But Mrs Chesterfield continued to stare at him with the same intense expression and an idea began to form in his mind. Whether he had thought of it himself or whether it had come from the figure standing opposite him, he couldn't say. Whatever the case, a remark made by his father was ringing in his brain. It was something Cicero had said after he had caught Nathaniel opening the letter from his grandfather. 'He may be a magistrate, but I am your father and I know my rights.'

'You think I should contact my grandfather, don't you?' Nathaniel asked her.

Slowly, Mrs Chesterfield nodded.

Nathaniel recalled his father's threat to throw him out of the window if he ever caught him reading his correspondence again but, under the pressure of Mrs Chesterfield's insistent gaze, he realised that he had no alternative. There would be no rest from the haunting until he had carried out her wishes.

Reluctantly, he got out of bed and crossed the room, passing far closer to the figure of Mrs Chesterfield than he might have wished. He tiptoed over to his father's bed and began searching through his clothes for the letter. It wasn't easy to find and Nathaniel began to fear that his father had destroyed it in a fit of rage. But at last he found it, shoved in his father's shoe for some reason.

His grandfather lived in a village in Kent. Nathaniel carefully memorised the address, then put the letter back where he had found it.

'You want me to write to him?' Nathaniel asked.

Mrs Chesterfield shook her head and glared at him. Waves of silent fury seemed to emanate from her.

'You want me to go and see him?'

She nodded her head.

'But I'll need to take a train and I haven't any money,' he told her.

She stared back at him, determination written across her face.

'All right,' he said. 'I'll do my best.'

She nodded and a moment later she was gone.

Nathaniel sighed. Now maybe he could get back to sleep, he said to himself. After all, he would have a long journey to make tomorrow.

14. WILLIAM MONKTON

Lily was standing at the kitchen sink the next morning, peeling potatoes for lunch, when there was a knock at the kitchen door.

'If it's that boy from the butcher's shop,' Mrs Simpson declared, 'tell him I don't want any more of his scrag end of lamb thank you very much. And you can say I'll be having a few words with his employer next time I'm in the High Street, while you're at it.'

But it wasn't the boy from the butcher's shop. It was Nathaniel.

'What's up?' Lily asked.

He told her about Mrs Chesterfield's appearance in the night. 'So I've got to go to Kent,' he concluded, 'and I was hoping you might come with me, for I'll never convince him on my own. Look how hard it was when we went to the Peelers.'

'What makes you think we'll have any more luck this time?' Lily asked.

Nathaniel shrugged. 'Nothing really. But I've got to try. It's what Mrs Chesterfield wants me to do. And it might be our only chance of saving Miss Sophie's life.'

Lily nodded. 'All right,' she said. 'Wait here. I'll be out again in five minutes.'

She ran straight up to her room, took out the tin box from under her bed and emptied the contents into her purse. That was all her savings gone. Then she went downstairs again and announced that she had to leave for Kent right away.

'What are you talking about?' Mrs Simpson said. 'You can't just walk out of the kitchen and leave everything. What's the master going to say?'

'I don't know,' Lily admitted.

'We shan't be able to cover up for you, you know.'

'I realise that.'

'You'll be out on your ear,' George added.

'I can't help it.'

'Yes you can,' George said. 'Just stay put. Problem solved.'

Lily shook her head. 'I wish it was as simple as that.'

'I don't understand what's come over you lately,' Mrs Simpson said.

'It's him, isn't it?' George said, nodding towards

the kitchen door where Nathaniel waited patiently. 'He's turned your head good and proper.'

Lily shook her head. 'It's not Nathaniel,' she said. 'It's Mrs Chesterfield.'

George and Mrs Simpson boggled at her.

'Mrs Chesterfield is dead,' George told her. 'We all went to the funeral, remember.'

'Of course I remember,' Lily said. 'But she wants me to go so I can try to save Miss Sophie's life. Oh look, there's no point in trying to explain. I just have to go and that's all there is to it.'

Suddenly, to her astonishment, Mrs Simpson burst into tears. 'I don't want to lose you, Lily,' she said. 'You're the best maid we've ever had.'

Lily went over to Mrs Simpson and gave her a hug. 'Thanks for everything, Mrs Simpson,' she said. Then she turned to George, and on impulse bent forwards and kissed him on the cheek. 'Wish me luck,' she said.

She left them standing there, Mrs Simpson with tears still rolling down her cheeks, and George with his hand raised to his cheek where she had kissed him and his mouth open, catching flies.

'Well, that's the end of my career,' she said as she set off down the road with Nathaniel.

'Can't you get a job in another house?' he asked.

Lily shook her head. 'Mr Chesterfield will never

give me a reference,' she told him.

'What are you going to do then?'

She shrugged. 'Hope for the best,' she said. 'What else can I do?'

'You'll be all right,' Nathaniel told her. 'My grandfather will sort things out. You wait and see.'

But he wasn't sure that he really believed it. Despite what Mr Monkton had written in his letter about wanting to see his grandson, Nathaniel couldn't help recalling that he was a man capable of quarrelling so fiercely with his daughter that he refused to talk to her for twelve years – and all because she chose to throw in her lot with a music-hall performer.

Victoria Station was swarming with people all hurrying in different directions, bumping into one another, apologising and then bumping into one another again. Even finding the ticket office was a difficult matter. But at last they had purchased two third-class tickets, identified the correct train, climbed on board and secured two seats towards the rear.

It didn't take long for the carriage to fill up with passengers: a fat clergyman with snuff stains down the front of his jacket sat opposite Lily, and a middle-aged clerk in a shiny suit with worn-out elbows sat next to him; then they were joined by a woman with a wicker box containing three kittens which mewed pitifully, and finally by an elderly man in knickerbockers and gaiters who beamed at everyone in the carriage and lifted his hat to the ladies.

At last, with a whistle from the guard, a wave of a green flag, and great clouds of sulphurous smoke, they were on their way.

Nathaniel had not expected the train to travel at such speed and he stared out of the window in amazement as the outskirts of London flashed by, soon giving way to green fields dotted with cows and sheep.

'I wonder what it would be like, living out in the countryside,' Lily said.

Nathaniel shook his head. 'Too much open space,' he replied. 'It makes me feel dizzy just looking at it.'

'I expect you'd get used to it,' Lily told him.

But Nathaniel was not so sure.

They passed country lanes and winding streams, thatched cottages and bustling inns, bare fields where the wheat had yet to raise its head above the black earth, orchards waiting for the warmth of spring to wake them from their winter sleep. Old men stood by the roadside puffing on clay pipes, small children waved, and dogs ran alongside, intent on chasing the train away from their territory.

After a couple of hours they pulled into the village of Lee, where Nathaniel's grandfather lived, and disembarked from the train. The station master told them that they would find Mr Monkton's residence about two miles outside the village on the Lemmington Road.

Nathaniel had not been sure what exactly to expect – a little cottage with roses growing around the door, perhaps. But, in fact, his grandfather's house was an imposing red-brick building set in its own grounds. He was conscious, as he rang the front doorbell, that he probably looked more like a beggar than a member of the family.

That was clearly the opinion of the butler who looked down his nose at Nathaniel when he asked to see Mr Monkton.

'My master does not receive visitors except by appointment,' he declared.

'I simply have to see him. It's a matter of life and death,' Nathaniel told him.

'That's as may be,' the butler replied, 'but I have my orders.' And with that, he closed the door in their faces.

Nathaniel had not come all this way to be turned back on the doorstep. He summoned up his courage and lifted the door knocker once more.

The door was opened a second time and the

butler's irate face peered through the gap. 'I've already told you, Mr Monkton cannot see anybody today,' he said sternly. 'Now kindly leave these premises immediately, or I shall have you forcibly removed.'

Nathaniel had just opened his mouth to tell the butler that he would like to see him try, when an elderly white-haired gentleman appeared behind him, leaning on a stick and looking very fierce.

'What is all this noise about, James?' he demanded.

'These two young people are demanding to see you, sir,' the butler told him. 'I've already explained that you do not see anyone except by appointment.'

'Grandfather,' Nathaniel said. 'It's me, Nathaniel.'

The old man stared back at him. His features, which only moments ago had been those of a stern and unyielding magistrate, seemed to dissolve and his face became that of a sad and lonely old man. 'What did you say?' he said, in a voice scarcely louder than a whisper.

'I said it's me, Nathaniel Wolfe. I've come all the way from London to see you. And this is my friend Miss Lily Campion.'

Mr Monkton pulled a handkerchief from his pocket and wiped his eye. For a moment he was too choked with emotion to talk. But finally he seemed to recover himself. Nodding his head vigorously, he beamed at them both. 'You'd better come in, then,' he said. He turned to the butler, who was looking entirely bewildered by the turn of events. 'James, tell Cook to make some tea. And we'd better have some sandwiches. And scones. With strawberry jam.' He turned back to Nathaniel with an expression of barely contained excitement. 'You do like strawberry jam, don't you?' he asked.

'When I can get it,' Nathaniel told him.

'Splendid!' Mr Monkton said. 'You'd better follow me then.'

He led the way into a very grand parlour, where they sat on leather armchairs beside a glowing fire. One thing that William Monkton was good at was listening. He didn't interrupt as Nathaniel and Lily took turns to tell their tale, except to urge them from time to time to help themselves from the plates of sandwiches and scones that were placed in front of them. When they were finished he sat in silence for a long time thinking about what he had heard.

Finally, Nathaniel said, 'Do you believe us?'

William Monkton did not answer directly. 'Last night I had a most peculiar dream,' he began. 'It seemed to me that a woman stood before me in the dock, all dressed in white. When I asked what the charge was against her nobody seemed to know, and the woman herself would not speak a word. But she looked at me as if she could see into my very soul, until I felt as if it was I who was on trial and not her.'

'It was my poor mistress! ' Lily said. 'It must have been!'

William Monkton nodded. 'Perhaps,' he agreed. 'However, I have to tell you that stories of ghostly visitation will not hold any sway in a court of law. If we are to act against this fellow, Chesterfield, we must first have proof.'

'But we haven't got time for proof!' Lily objected. 'Miss Sophie only has a few days left to live.'

'So it would seem,' the old man replied. 'But there is nothing further that can be done tonight. I shall decide what course of action to pursue tomorrow morning.'

Lily opened her mouth to urge him not to delay but he held up a finger to silence her. 'Before we go any further Nathaniel must tell me about his life for the last twelve years,' he insisted. 'I have a great deal of catching up to do.'

Nathaniel summoned up everything he could remember of his early life – watching his parents perform from the wings of a stage; his mother teaching him his letters and her gradual withdrawal as illness overcame her (there were tears in his grandfather's eyes as he listened to this); his father's unsuccessful attempts to continue his career as an entertainer and his decision to adopt the guise of a medium. He spoke about Cicero's drunken rages and his mounting debts. The old man listened to it all without comment.

William Monkton was a very different sort of a person from Cicero Wolfe, and it was not hard to see why the two of them had not hit it off. Cicero was a showman, given to grand gestures and fond of the sound of his own voice. When he had money he liked to flaunt it; when he was broke he preferred to ignore the fact. He looked down on those whom he considered less knowledgable than himself and he envied those who were more successful.

William Monkton, on the other hand, was a very private man. Despite thirty years spent as a magistrate, he still preferred to keep his thoughts to himself unless specifically required to comment. He never worried about money, though of course that was only possible because he had a great deal of it. He looked down only on those whom he considered morally degenerate: the miserable collection of thieves, bullies and ruffians who regularly stood before him in the dock. He could be hard on those who would not admit their guilt but he always sought to be fair in his judgements. Nevertheless, most criminals shuddered when they heard that they were up before 'The Monk'.

But sitting in his armchair, listening to the story of Nathaniel's life, he was a very different man from the one who struck fear into the felons of Kent. 'Do you know what the most important lesson life teaches us is?' he asked, when Nathaniel finally reached the end of his tale.

Nathaniel shook his head.

'You must always be prepared to admit when you have made a mistake.' William Monkton shook his head sadly. 'I have been an utter fool,' he said bitterly. 'What should have been the best years of my life have been poisoned by my own ridiculous pride and stubbornness.'

'It wasn't just one-sided,' Nathaniel pointed out.

'True,' the old man agreed. 'But it was my refusal to welcome your father into the family that began the quarrel. In those days I was so certain of my own judgement and I believed I knew exactly the kind of man your father was – vain, feckless and irresponsible.'

'That's the truth,' Nathaniel told him. 'That's exactly what Cicero is like.'

'But it isn't the whole story, is it? Your mother loved him. Why? Because she saw something special in him. A kind of poetry, that was what she told me. "Cicero brings his own imagination to life." Those were her very words. But I refused to listen. All I was interested in was whether or not he could provide her with a respectable life.'

'You were trying to do your duty,' Nathaniel told him.

'Duty isn't everything,' his grandfather replied. 'It has taken me all these years to understand that. It is more important to open your heart to your fellow man.' He sat in silence, staring into the fire for a long time. At last he looked up and smiled. 'But I thank the Lord that it is not too late. You have come back to me, Nathaniel, and I shall do everything in my power to ensure that the bonds between us are never broken again.'

He turned to Lily, who had been sitting in silence throughout all of this. 'Thank you for your patience, Miss Campion. As you see, I am an old man and old men are slow. But I have made up my mind. I have been given a chance, even at the eleventh hour, to do a little good in the world and I intend to seize it. Do not fear for your young mistress any longer. We will put a stop to this villain, Chesterfield. You have my word upon it.'

15. FLOWN THE COOP

That night Nathaniel slept in the biggest and softest bed he had ever seen. He woke once with no idea where he was. Then he remembered, smiled to himself and settled back into sleep. There were no unexplained chills and no ghostly visitations to contend with. He did not have to put up with Cicero snoring or the sound of mice in the wainscoting, and he woke up feeling more refreshed than he could ever remember.

Breakfast was rather an ordeal. The food was wonderful – bacon and eggs, kippers and kedgeree, toast and jam, tea and coffee and baskets piled high with fruit. But there were so many different knives, forks and spoons and Nathaniel had no idea what to do with any of them. He was aware, also, from the looks his grandfather gave him from time to time, that he was bolting his food. But never before had such a banquet been placed in front of him and for all he knew it might never happen again. So he intended to make the most of the opportunity.

It was easier for Lily, since she understood how meals were served to gentlemen and ladies. She knew the difference between a fish knife and a fruit knife and the correct order in which food should be eaten. But even she was not used to being waited on. She had to resist the urge to hand round the plates, pour the tea and spring up to clear away the dirty dishes.

When they had eaten all they could manage William Monkton announced that they would be taking the very next train to London. 'Which gives us exactly twenty minutes to get to the station.'

'It took us longer than that to walk here last night,' Nathaniel pointed out in dismay.

'We will travel to the station in my carriage,' his grandfather assured him.

What a different world rich people lived in, Nathaniel thought to himself. They didn't have to walk anywhere if they didn't want to. If his grandfather and his father had not quarrelled he might have lived like that for the past twelve years.

It was the same butler who opened the door for them as they left the house. He gave not the slightest indication that he had considered Nathaniel and Lily to be little more than vagabonds the previous evening. Nathaniel was tempted to make a face at him behind his grandfather's back, but he thought better of it. You may not be a gentleman's son, he told himself, but you're a gentleman's grandson and you'd better start acting like it.

They travelled first class to London and had the compartment to themselves. William Monkton took the opportunity to ask more questions about Lily's household. For some reason he seemed particularly interested in the arrangement of rooms. 'You say the back parlour, where your mistress used to play the piano, is really one and the same room as the front parlour?'

'Yes sir. It's just dividing doors that separates them.'

'And Mr Chesterfield's study is further down the hall?'

'That's right.'

'Would you say he was a strong man, physically I mean?'

Lily nodded. 'I should think so. He's tall. Not really muscular, but wiry. And he gives the impression he's not afraid of anyone.'

William Monkton nodded. He turned back to Nathaniel. 'First and foremost we must visit your father,' he declared. 'Naturally, he will be concerned about your welfare and he will want to be reassured that you have come to no harm.'

Nathaniel doubted this very much but he did not like to disillusion his grandfather any further about Cicero's character.

'Moreover,' the old man continued, 'we may have need of assistance if this fellow Chesterfield is as dangerous as you suggest. Your father will provide us with the necessary support.'

Nathaniel grew less and less talkative as the train drew nearer to London. He was dreading the meeting between the two men. Despite his grandfather's best intentions, he knew that Cicero would not be prepared to let bygones be bygones. Nor would he be even remotely interested in apprehending Mr Chesterfield. But this was something that William Monkton was going to have to find out for himself.

Lily, too, was deeply worried. Before they had gone to bed the night before, Mr Monkton had insisted on giving her money to replace what she had spent on their journey from London. So at least she was not entirely penniless. But she had no idea what the future held for her. Either Mr Chesterfield's guilt would be confirmed, or he would turn out to be innocent. In either event, she could not see how there could possibly be a job for her afterwards.

As the fields gave way to houses, even Mr Monkton seemed grim and apprehensive. He stared out of the window in silence, turning over in his mind what had to be done. The mission that had seemed so clear in his mind when they set out earlier that morning was starting to appear altogether more daunting as the reality grew nearer. He was an old man, he reminded himself, and despite his promise to Lily the night before, he was much less confident than he appeared. He had been given a chance to make amends for his mistakes. He only hoped that he was up to the task.

They took a hansom cab from Victoria Station. Nathaniel saw his grandfather looking out of the window and frowning as the streets grew narrower and more dingy, the closer they got to Stepney. He tried to see the area through his grandfather's eyes and he supposed it must have seemed like the most appalling collection of slums. 'It's not as bad as it looks,' he said. 'There's good people out there as well as villains.'

'No doubt,' his grandfather replied, but his face had reverted to the stern countenance of the magistrate rather than the kindly features of a grandfather.

As they drew nearer to Mrs Bizzantine's lodging house, Nathaniel's apprehension increased. A small crowd gathered as they got down from the cab – such means of transport being rare enough in these parts of the city. Mr Monkton instructed the cab driver to wait and they walked up to the front door, Nathaniel in the lead and his grandfather bringing up the rear.

Mrs Bizzantine herself met him at the front door, arms folded across her chest and an expression on her face that might have stopped a clock and turned back a funeral.

'I don't know what you think you're doing, turning up here like this,' she told him, her voice trembling with anger.

'I don't understand what you mean,' Nathaniel said.

'Oh, you don't?' Mrs Bizzantine said, scornfully. 'Well, I'll tell you, since you're so ill-informed. Your old man has done a bunk.'

'What do you mean?'

'Exactly what I say. He's scarpered, vanished, flown the coop.'

'I'm sure he'll be back,' Nathaniel protested.

'Is that right? Then perhaps you can explain why he's taken everything with him what wasn't nailed down: plates, knives, forks, spoons, blankets. All of it my property.'

Nathaniel was not prepared for this. 'But where's he gone?' he demanded.

'I really couldn't care less where he's gone,' Mrs Bizzantine went on. 'What I want to know is, who's going to pay for what he's taken?'

Mr Monkton stepped forward. 'If you will make a list of what is outstanding, I shall settle it immediately,' he told her.

Mrs Bizzantine seemed to notice him for the first time. 'And who might you be?' she demanded.

'Nathaniel's grandfather.'

'I see. Well, I hope you realise that I'm talking about six weeks' rent as well as what's gone missing.'

William Monkton nodded. 'Just put it down in writing,' he told her. 'You shall have the money immediately.'

Mrs Bizzantine looked as if she did not quite know what to say. Her features seemed to go through a whole variety of expressions. Finally, she recovered herself enough to respond, 'I can't write.'

Mr Monkton looked unsurprised. 'How much are we talking about?' he asked.

Mrs Bizzantine thought for a moment. Her lips moved silently, as though calculating, then she named a sum.

'That's too much!' Nathaniel protested.

'It is of no consequence,' William Monkton told him. He took out his wallet and handed over the money to Mrs Bizzantine.

'Much obliged I'm sure,' she told him, her earlier belligerence entirely forgotten.

After she had gone back inside, Jeremiah appeared, looking sympathetic. Nathaniel introduced him to his grandfather and the two men shook hands.

'Shame about your father,' Jeremiah said, as though he was commiserating with Nathaniel on Cicero's death.

'I wonder where he's gone,' Nathaniel said.

'Well, wherever it is, he's taken Mrs Gaunt with him,' Jeremiah told him.

'Mrs Gaunt!'

''Fraid so. I come across the two of them last night, sharing a bottle of gin, and your father told me he was going to resurrect his music-hall career. "Mrs Gaunt and I will be treading the boards as a double-act",' Jeremiah added, in a passable imitation of Cicero's most florid tones.

'Did he say anything about me?' Nathaniel asked.

'Well, I did ask him if he had any plans for you,' Jeremiah said. 'But he reckoned you was old enough to look after yourself.'

'It seems there is no point in us remaining here any further,' William Monkton announced. 'We have work to do elsewhere.'

'I'll bid you farewell then,' Jeremiah said. 'And I'll say thanks, too. You've proved a true friend to young

Nathaniel here when there's others what might have more cause to do.'

Mr Monkton nodded. 'I hope I may do more for him in the days to come. But perhaps you and I need not part. You look like a man who can take care of himself, someone who wouldn't be easily frightened of a ruffian. Would I be right about that?'

Jeremiah nodded. 'You could say so, and you wouldn't be all that wide of the mark.'

'Then we stand in need of your help.'

'I'll do what I can,' Jeremiah promised.

'Let us waste no more time,' Mr Monkton said. He led the way back to the hansom and they set off for the Chesterfield residence.

'So what are we going to do when we arrive?' Lily asked. She had stood by in silence while Nathaniel and his grandfather negotiated with Mrs Bizzantine and had said nothing when Mr Monkton had asked Jeremiah to join them. But now they were headed for the house where until yesterday morning she had worked as a maid since she was nine years old, and she felt it was time that she was consulted. 'We can't just knock on the door and ask Mr Chesterfield if he'd please stop poisoning Miss Sophie,' she went on. 'At least, I don't think he'd take very kindly to it if we did.'

'I have been thinking about that,' Mr Monkton replied.

'Well I'm glad somebody has,' she told him. 'What's your plan then?'

16. FACE TO FACE

Mr Chesterfield took out the key to his front door and let himself in. He'd had a worrying day. First there was the news that Lily had disappeared. Neither George nor Mrs Simpson seemed to have the faintest idea what had happened to her. Now he would have to arrange for someone to take her place and that was not going to be easy. Good servants were hard to find. Most of them were lazy, workshy layabouts who only wanted a roof over their heads and three square meals a day.

Then he had gone to see Bulstrode to make sure that everything had gone smoothly with regard to Maggot Harris, and the stupid fool had told him that people had been calling at the funeral parlour asking questions. A boy and a girl he'd said, though he wasn't able to give any sort of a description. Of course Bulstrode hadn't had the sense to ask their names or the nature of their interest in the deceased, he'd just turned them away without finding out a thing. It might mean nothing, Mr Chesterfield told himself. After all, the Peelers had been satisfied, but it was unsettling, and he didn't like to be unsettled.

'Begging your pardon, sir?'

It was George, standing in front of him with that idiotic expression on his face. He'd always wondered whether there wasn't something slightly wrong with that boy in the brain department – slow on the uptake, gormless expression. Pity *he* wasn't the one who had gone missing.

'What is it?' Mr Chesterfield demanded.

'There's a boy waiting to see you in the front parlour, sir.'

Mr Chesterfield found himself experiencing a mixture of bewilderment and a creeping sense of panic. 'What boy?' he demanded.

'He says his name is Nathaniel Wolfe, sir.'

'Nathaniel Wolfe? I know no boy of that name. You had no right to show him into the parlour. Tell him I'm too busy to see him and send him on his way.'

It was a simple enough instruction. What was a footman for, after all, if he couldn't deal with an unwanted visitor? But George just stood there with that half-witted expression on his face.

'He said it was most urgent, sir. In connection with the death of a Mr Harris.'

The shock was like someone throwing a bucket of

water over him. He stood in the hallway, staring at George as if he had been paralysed. Finally, he managed to come back to his senses. What are you doing? he said to himself. You might as well write out a confession and hand it over to that imbecile. Pull yourself together, for goodness' sake.

'Very well, I'll speak to him myself. You can go.'

He could have sworn that George was smiling as he turned and walked off down the hall. Does he know something? Mr Chesterfield asked himself. But it wasn't possible. He was just getting jumpy. It was the shock, that was all. But who was the boy in the parlour and what did he know? He must be the one who had been to see Bulstrode. But that didn't mean the game was up. Just behave normally, Mr Chesterfield told himself. Find out what the boy wants and get rid of him as quickly as you can.

He opened the door of the parlour and stepped inside. A boy of about twelve years old was sitting in one of the armchairs. He stood up when Mr Chesterfield entered the room. There was something vaguely familiar about him, but Mr Chesterfield could not say where he had seen him before.

'Nathaniel Wolfe, I believe?' Mr Chesterfield began.

'That's right,' Nathaniel said.

There was something insolent about his tone but

Mr Chesterfield decided to ignore it. All in good time, he told himself.

'And what was it you wanted to see me about?' he asked.

'The death of Maggot Harris,' Nathaniel told him.

'I'm sorry, I don't think I know anyone of that name,' Mr Chesterfield replied. 'I think you must have made a mistake.'

Nathaniel shook his head. 'The mistake is yours, Mr Chesterfield,' he said.

'I beg your pardon?'

'Your maid, Lily, saw you talking to him in your study last Wednesday.'

'I see,' Mr Chesterfield said. 'This is what Lily has been getting up to, is it? Well, she's not my maid any longer, I can assure you of that.' He drew himself up to his full height and scowled down at the boy. 'Now I suggest you leave this house immediately, before I throw you out.'

The extraordinary thing was that the boy seemed entirely unabashed. He didn't make the slightest move to go. On the contrary he carried on in the same quietly insolent manner, as if he had not heard Mr Chesterfield threaten to throw him out.

'It's not just Lily,' he went on. 'It's well known that you paid the bills for Maggot's funeral. Only you should have gone through his pockets before you left him down in the sewers, because he had a receipt from the chemist for six pennyworth of arsenic in one of them.'

It was all Mr Chesterfield could do to keep his mouth from dropping open. How had the boy discovered all this? What else did he know? Calm down, he said to himself. He made his voice silky with menace. 'And where is that receipt now?' he demanded.

'I have it here,' Nathaniel told him.

Mr Chesterfield smiled and relief flooded through his body. What a fool the boy was! A moment ago he had held all the cards. Now he had thrown them away. The receipt was in the boy's pocket, the boy was in his parlour – the situation was under Mr Chesterfield's control.

'I'm afraid you have made a very big mistake,' Mr Chesterfield told him. 'Do you think I'm going to let a child get in the way of my plans?' He shook his head slowly. 'I can silence you just as I silenced Maggot Harris.' He stepped closer to Nathaniel. He knew exactly what he was going to do. He would squeeze the life out of the boy without anyone hearing a thing.

But at that very moment the dividing doors which separated the two parlours were folded back. Two men whom he had never set eyes on before stepped into the room. One was elderly and white-haired, the other younger and powerfully built. They took hold of him and the elderly fellow spoke. 'Under my authority as a magistrate, I am arresting you upon suspicion of murder and of attempted murder,' he said.

Mr Chesterfield gave a cry of rage. He had been tricked! But he would not allow them to take him in his own front parlour. He aimed a savage kick at the elderly man, grabbed hold of the boy and hurled him at the heavily built fellow. Then he sprang out of the room, down the hall and out the front door.

17. UNDERGROUND

William Monkton was lying on the ground clutching his leg, pain written across his face.

'Are you all right, Grandfather?' Nathaniel asked, anxiously.

'Never mind me,' his grandfather hissed. 'Get after him!'

Nathaniel nodded. He rushed out of the house with Jeremiah at his heels and they were just in time to glimpse Mr Chesterfield disappearing round a corner at the end of the street. Without a word, they set off in pursuit.

But Mr Chesterfield was running for his life, and it was no easy matter keeping him in sight. He neither paused for breath nor to get his bearings. Soon he had left behind the more salubrious area where the Chesterfields' house was situated and was heading for the most notorious slums in the East End, the area known as The Rookeries. Many a criminal had evaded capture by disappearing into this warren of tiny alleyways.

Even Nathaniel nearly hesitated to follow him here. The streets in which Mrs Bizzantine had her lodging house were bright and airy boulevards in comparison to this narrow, twisting, filthy maze. Rotten timber propped up crumbling masonry, windows were patched with newspaper or rags, the broken cobbles were strewn with rotting vegetables, old straw and dung. The Rookeries was the very lowest rung on the great ladder of London society. The only place beneath it was death itself and there were many who considered that a more desirable destination.

But Mr Chesterfield did not think twice. He plunged into the heart of The Rookeries like a netted fish thrown back into water. He's been here before, Nathaniel thought to himself as he struggled to keep pace with his quarry. He knows this area like the back of his hand. And then it came to him – this was where Mr Chesterfield had come from! Before ever he was a gentleman, Lily's master had been a Rookeries Boy.

He twisted and turned, ducked and dodged, leapt over fences and scrambled through courtyards. Hens ran across the street clucking and flapping their wings in fright; dogs bared their teeth and barked at him; cats shot into doorways; one old woman carrying a bundle of firewood was knocked clean off her feet and lay on the ground cursing and spitting at him; a group of children threw lumps of mud in his direction; but Mr Chesterfield stopped for no one.

Then at last he made an error of judgement. He turned into a blind alley, at the end of which was a high brick wall.

'Now we've got him,' Jeremiah said as Mr Chesterfield turned to face them, like a cornered animal. There was a brief moment when each side stood staring at the other. Then Mr Chesterfield began running towards them. Nathaniel and Jeremiah braced themselves to catch him but he stopped halfway down the alley and turned towards the wall once more. He had only been giving himself space to make a run at it.

Now he reached the wall and threw himself upwards. Somehow he managed to grasp the top and he hung there for a moment before one of his feet found a gap in the masonry and, spider-like, he clambered over. He paused at the top to look contemptuously at his pursuers. Then he was gone.

'He ain't getting away that easy!' Jeremiah cried as they reached the wall a moment later. He clasped his hands together and held them out towards Nathaniel. 'Put your foot in there!' he ordered.

Nathaniel did as he was told and Jeremiah lifted him high enough to reach the top line of bricks. He pulled himself up until he was sitting astride the wall. On the other side he could see a small square of ground and then the back of a tenement block, but there was no sign of Mr Chesterfield.

'Can you see him?' Jeremiah asked.

'No.'

'Help me up.'

Nathaniel reached down and Jeremiah took his hand, pulling himself upwards with such force that he nearly caused Nathaniel to lose his balance. But Nathaniel clung on with his knees while Jeremiah got a foothold, and at last he too was sitting on the top. Then he jumped down on the other side and helped Nathaniel to the ground after him.

'Where do you think he went?' Nathaniel asked.

'Underground,' Jeremiah replied, nodding towards a set of steps that Nathaniel had not spotted, leading downwards in a corner of the yard. Jeremiah reached into his pocket and brought out a candle and a box of lucifers. 'A tosher is never without a light,' he said with a wink. Then he lit the candle and led the way down the steps.

They found themselves in a low brick room with a beaten earth floor and no windows. At the furthest end was a gully with an opening in the wall behind it that was just about Nathaniel's height. It had obviously once been used as a cesspit for the filth and waste of the tenement. The opening behind it would no doubt lead into the sewers below the city.

'That's where he's gone,' Jeremiah said.

'What are we going to do?' Nathaniel asked.

'Go after him, of course. If he thinks he can lose us down here, he's got another thing coming. A tosher is at home underground. Come on.'

With that he stepped into the gully, bent almost double, and led the way through the opening behind it. Nervously, Nathaniel followed.

The opening behind the gulley led into a narrow brick tunnel. In the centre of the tunnel was a trickle of water that soon grew into a stream as it was fed by dozens of little tributaries issuing from the sides at regular intervals. The ground beneath their feet was slippery and treacherous but it was the smell that Nathaniel noticed most of all. The further along the tunnel they went, the stronger it grew, closing in on them like a fog.

It was as if all the filthiest odours of London had been boiled down in some great cauldron and trapped underground. Nathaniel could smell unwashed bodies, rotten meat, fish guts and cabbage, the sulphurous reek of match factories and the thick, cloying stench of breweries, the acrid fumes from the lime pits, and the dizzying vapours of glue-makers. The resulting cocktail seemed to seep inside his brain so that he staggered as he walked and a cold sweat broke out on his forehead.

But Jeremiah was entirely undeterred and there was nothing Nathaniel could do but try to keep up and stay alert at all times. It would be a fatal mistake, he realised, to lose his footing and slip into those turgid waters. The very thought of it made him shudder.

Suddenly Jeremiah stopped and seized him by the arm. 'Look up ahead!' he whispered.

Nathaniel had been focusing all his attention on where he planted his feet, but now he raised his eyes and saw, far in advance of them, like a will-o'-the-wisp, the faint gleam of another candle.

'We've got him in our sights now,' Jeremiah said, setting off once more.

They pressed on with greater speed and, to Nathaniel's relief, the going became easier. The tunnel grew both wider and taller so that it was possible to stand up straight as they went. From time to time they came to a junction where two or more branches of the sewers met, and it always seemed to Nathaniel that any one of the options that presented itself was just as likely as any other. But Jeremiah did not hesitate, and sure enough, after each branch had been navigated, they would see the flickering candlelight up ahead of them once more.

In many places the walls of the tunnel were covered with fungus, a leprous, spongy growth that Nathaniel shrank from instinctively. Once or twice he could not avoid brushing against it and its wet, slimy texture, uncomfortably reminiscent of human flesh, filled him with disgust.

In other places thin cones of some chalky substance hung from the ceiling, like icicles, and they were forced to creep beneath them. All the time the stream beside which they walked grew larger and larger until it was more like an underground river, its surface a mass of foamy scum, the sound of its current growing ever louder and echoing in the empty spaces of the underground world like the souls of lost spirits crying out for comfort.

How Jeremiah worked in this place every day, Nathaniel could not imagine. It was the closest thing he could imagine to Hell. There was nothing wholesome down here – no sunlight, no fresh air and no plants or flowers – unless you counted the fungus that lined the tunnel walls. But there was animal life. From time to time Nathaniel caught a glimpse of sleek brown bodies scuttling from shadow to shadow, or he spied of a pair of glittering eyes watching him from a distance, sizing him up no doubt, waiting to see whether he would give up the chase and just lie down and die. He remembered what Mrs Marble had told him about Maggot Harris, how the rats had chewed off one of his ears. And he remembered what Jeremiah had said, that from time to time someone disappeared in the sewers and how the other toshers would say that Shallow Jack had taken him. He began to long to be up on the surface again, instead of endlessly travelling these miserable tunnels like a worm in a rotten apple.

Suddenly Jeremiah stopped and seemed to sniff the air like a dog looking for a scent.

'What is it?' Nathaniel asked him.

'A storm's coming,' Jeremiah answered.

'Are you sure?' How Jeremiah could possibly identify the scent of impending rain down here in this great soup of smells, Nathaniel was not able to imagine, but Jeremiah looked utterly certain.

'It's not far away, neither,' he said. 'We have to get above ground as quickly as possible.'

'What about Mr Chesterfield?'

'We'll have to forget about him.'

'But he'll get away!'

'Can't be helped. Come on. No time to lose.'

He turned down a narrow side tunnel which Nathaniel would have walked straight by without noticing and before very long they were stooping once again as the distance between floor and ceiling grew smaller. They came to a T-junction and Jeremiah stopped, frowning.

'What's the matter?' Nathaniel asked, nervously.

Jeremiah said nothing, but his lips moved silently, as though counting. At last he made up his mind and took the left-hand fork.

'You do know where you're going, don't you?' Nathaniel asked.

'I've a good idea,' Jeremiah said, but his voice did not possess its usual certainty.

It was impossible to tell whether they were going upwards or downwards and Nathaniel's anxiety grew as they went further and further without any sign that they were approaching an exit. Suddenly he heard a distant rumbling noise.

'What was that?' he asked.

'Thunder,' Jeremiah told him. 'Storm's broken up above ground. Can't you feel it?'

Nathaniel realised that he could. The temperature had dropped considerably and he could sense the increased moisture in the air.

'It's a big one by the feel of it,' Jeremiah said. 'We'll know all about it soon enough. Come on, we must hurry.'

It was soon clear what Jeremiah meant by 'knowing all about it'. The stream of water that flowed down the middle of the tunnel began rising rapidly and flowing with much greater speed. Soon it had reached the top of the channel and was lapping over the bank on either side.

'How high does it rise?' Nathaniel asked.

'It can fill the tunnel,' Jeremiah told him.

They were splashing through water that was up to their ankles now and Nathaniel was struggling to fight back a sense of panic. What if Jeremiah's knowledge of the sewers was not as thorough as he imagined? What if the water continued to rise until they lost their footing? What if the candle flame was extinguished and the sheer force of the current washed them away along miles of dark and featureless tunnels? What if they held their breaths until their lungs were ready to burst but finally had to open their mouths and let that tide of filth and scum come pouring in to fill their lungs?

Jeremiah stopped. 'Here we are,' he said.

With an immense sense of relief, Nathaniel saw that he was standing beside a vertical shaft. A metal ladder fixed to the wall led upwards towards a grating, through which the light of day was clearly visible.

'You go first,' Jeremiah told him. 'When you get to the top, put both your hands under the grating and push.'

Gratefully, Nathaniel took hold of the ladder and climbed up the shaft. When he reached the top he put his hands under the grating and shoved. But it wouldn't move! The elation he had felt only a moment earlier disappeared, replaced by panic. 'I can't open it!' he called back.

'Come on down,' Jeremiah told him.

Unhappily, Nathaniel descended the ladder. Even in the short space of time it had taken him to climb up and down the ladder, the water level in the tunnel had risen. Now it was halfway up to his knee.

'I'll see what I can do,' Jeremiah told him. He climbed quickly up the ladder and Nathaniel could see him struggling to move the grating.

He wasn't going to succeed, Nathaniel realised. For one reason or another the grating was stuck, and they were trapped like the rats in Jeremiah's wooden cages.

But Jeremiah gave a mighty groan and suddenly the grating moved aside. 'Come on!' Jeremiah called.

Nathaniel needed no second invitation. He swarmed up the ladder and found himself standing blinking in the daylight beside Jeremiah. It was pouring with rain but he didn't care. He turned to Jeremiah, who was grinning happily at him. 'That was a close one,' Jeremiah told him. He bent down and replaced the grating.

'We'd best find our way back to your grandfather,' he added when he had straightened up.

Nathaniel nodded. He had no idea where they were. But Jeremiah seemed to know. He set off down the road and Nathaniel followed. Now that the danger of drowning in the sewers was past, he remembered what they had been doing down there in the first place.

'What about Mr Chesterfield?' he asked. 'Do you think he got away?'

'I shouldn't worry about him any longer if I was you,' Jeremiah said. 'There weren't no exits for a very long way where he was headed. No, if you want my opinion, our friend Mr Chesterfield is probably shaking hands with Shallow Jack at this very moment.'

18. A VERY IMPORTANT PERSON

It was a month since Cicero had disappeared, a month during which Nathaniel had become used to a very different way of life at his grandfather's house in Kent. In that time he had learned, among other things, how to sit and soak in a bath of hot water, how to wear different clothes every day of the week, and how to eat his food like a gentleman. Some parts of his new identity he found harder to get used to than others, like sitting back and waiting while servants fetched and carried for him. Some parts he suspected he would never be very good at, like riding a horse or making polite conversation at a dinner party. But, all things considered, he was making good progress. At least, that was the opinion of his grandfather.

Nevertheless, the sights and sounds of London

never really vanished from his mind. He could not forget about Lily and Jeremiah and Mrs Bizzantine's lodging house for long. London was in his blood and he missed everything about it, even the smells.

So when his grandfather announced that the time had come for them to return, he was filled with excitement, but also with trepidation because what lay ahead was not just a simple visit to the East End and a chance to catch up with his old friends. Nathaniel Wolfe was now a famous person – his story had been the talk of London for weeks and his new-found status brought responsibilities with it.

Not that he had sought notoriety. He had wanted the whole story hushed up, but that had proved impossible. As a magistrate, his grandfather had been obliged to report his part in the proceedings to the authorities, and when Mr Chesterfield's body had been washed up on the banks of the Thames, the story had begun to leak out into the public domain, thanks largely to one man – Mortimer Pinkus. As soon as he heard about Mr Chesterfield's death Mr Pinkus had put two and two together. He had come looking for Lily and Nathaniel and soon the newspapers were full of reports of the Stepney Poisoner, the kitchen-maid and the magistrate's long-lost grandson. The public were fascinated to hear about messages from beyond the grave.

Everyone, from the humblest chimney sweep to Members of Parliament, was asking questions. Word of what had happened had even reached Buckingham Palace, where Her Majesty Queen Victoria had been living in seclusion ever since the death of her beloved Prince Albert.

It was said that the Queen had taken the most extraordinary interest in the case, that she read every newspaper report, that she had spoken personally to Mortimer Pinkus, and that she had talked of little else for days. All this Nathaniel had heard from his grandfather, who had connections among the highest levels of London society. Finally, the very thing that Nathaniel had been dreading had happened. He had been summoned to the Palace.

It was a very great honour, his grandfather told him and, of course, Nathaniel could see that. But only a few weeks earlier he had not known which knife and fork to use to eat his dinner. How could he possibly negotiate an interview with the most important person in the land?

They took the early train into London and then a hansom cab to an inn where his grandfather had booked rooms for them. A splendid luncheon was waiting for them but Nathaniel could eat none of it. The food might as well have been made of sawdust. 'What will I say to her?' he kept asking his grandfather.

'You will say nothing until you are spoken to,' his grandfather replied. 'And anything you do say will be the truth. Add nothing and take nothing away. As long as you stick to these simple rules, you cannot go wrong.'

But it was easy enough for his grandfather to say that. For years Nathaniel had assisted in a fraud which his father had perpetrated upon some of the poorest and most vulnerable people in the country. He had tried to stand up to his father, of course, but he had failed. Would Her Majesty understand that? Would she realise what kind of man his father was? After all, no one had ever dangled *her* out of the window by her legs and threatened to drop her onto the cobblestones below.

He wished he could have brought Lily along to help him tell the story. But the Queen had not wanted to see Lily. She was only interested in Nathaniel for some reason.

'You need not trouble yourself,' his grandfather said, as they sat in the dining room of the inn while the servants removed the remains of their meal. 'I have heard it said that Her Majesty is a very good judge of character.'

But that was exactly what worried Nathaniel. Would the Queen look at him and see a boy from the gutters of the East End, someone whose father had been a drunkard and a gambler, a fraudster and an impostor. Would she think he had not done enough to turn his father from a life of deceit?

Even as he was thinking this, the innkeeper entered the room. He was a stout, red-faced man with a loud voice and a hearty manner, but now he looked extremely solemn. 'There is a gentleman here to collect Master Nathaniel Wolfe,' he said.

Nathaniel swallowed nervously. He turned to his grandfather who smiled encouragingly back at him. 'Just be yourself, Nathaniel,' he said.

But who am I? Nathaniel wondered as he got up and followed the innkeeper out of the room.

The gentleman who was waiting to see him was tall and thin. He wore a frock coat and waistcoat and carried a top hat under his arm. He introduced himself as Sir Frederick Ponsonby, Private Secretary to Her Majesty Queen Victoria. There was something about the way he spoke that suggested he was not particularly pleased to be dealing with a person like Nathaniel.

'I want to make one thing clear to you,' he said as he led the way out into the street where a gleaming carriage bearing the royal coat of arms stood waiting. 'Anything that Her Majesty says to you or anything that you say to Her Majesty is to remain utterly confidential. Do you know what that means?'

'I'm not to tell a soul,' Nathaniel replied.

'Precisely. Were you to give the slightest hint of what passes between you to the gentlemen of the press for example, the consequences could be very grave indeed.'

'I know how to keep my mouth shut,' Nathaniel told him. 'You don't have to make threats.'

Sir Frederick nodded. 'Good. Then we understand each other.'

They climbed into the coach and set off for the Palace. For most of the journey Sir Frederick remained silent, apparently deep in thought while Nathaniel stared out of the window at the grand houses they drove past. He had been to this part of London before, of course, but he had never looked out at it through a carriage window. He had always felt that he did not belong in such streets, that he ought to get back to the East End as quickly as possible before a Peeler arrested him on suspicion of some crime or another. But this afternoon, he reminded himself, he had a right to be here. He had been summoned by the Queen herself.

As the carriage turned into the gates of the Palace, however, Sir Frederick came out of his reverie. 'I have one last thing to say to you, Nathaniel Wolfe,' he announced, 'and it is this. You must be aware that Her Majesty has been most deeply distressed by the loss of her husband, Prince Albert. Indeed, it has affected her most grievously. Consequently, you may find that some of her questions are of an unusual nature. She has become…how shall I put this? Well, she has become intrigued by the possibility of being reconciled with the Prince. In short, she has developed a deep interest in the afterlife.' He sounded as if he did not approve of the Queen's interest. 'This may sound like a very strange thing to say to a boy before he visits the most powerful person in the country,' he continued. 'Nevertheless, I must ask you not to take advantage of Her Majesty.'

Nathaniel gave him a long look. He did not like Sir Frederick. He found him cold and distant and it was obvious that he looked down on ordinary people and found dealing with them distasteful. Yet Nathaniel felt that he was an honest man who had the best interests of his queen and his country at heart. So he nodded at last. 'I know my duty, sir,' he said.

To his disappointment, he was not taken into the Palace through the main entrance. Instead Sir Frederick led him through a side door so insignificant that Nathaniel did not even notice it until they were standing right in front of it. Then they walked along what seemed like miles of red-carpeted corridors, up an enormous stairway and down another set of corridors. There was no time to marvel at the fine furniture that stood everywhere, no time to look at oneself in the huge mirrors or study the splendid paintings that hung on every wall. Sir Frederick kept up a brisk pace. From time to time they passed liveried servants in powdered wigs who stood as motionless as statues in front of closed doors. But no one asked them their business or made any attempt to detain them.

At last Sir Frederick stopped outside a set of double-doors which seemed to Nathaniel no different from a dozen similar entrances. He spoke to one of the two servants who stood outside. 'Would you be so kind as to tell Her Majesty that I have brought Master Wolfe to see her?' he said.

The servant nodded and disappeared inside the room. A moment later he reappeared and told them to follow him. Sir Frederick went first, then Nathaniel, butterflies fluttering violently in his stomach.

Queen Victoria was sitting at a very ordinary writing desk in the centre of the room. Clad all in black, she was a great deal smaller than Nathaniel had expected. He bowed as low as he could without toppling forwards.

'Please stand up straight, Master Wolfe,' Queen Victoria said.

Nathaniel straightened up.

'It is our wish that you should be put entirely at your ease,' she continued.

'Thank you, Your Majesty.'

'Do sit down.' She pointed to a chair beside her own.

'Sir Frederick will leave us for the time being.'

'Of course, Ma'am,' Sir Frederick agreed, but he did not look as if he was entirely pleased with this arrangement.

'Oh, and Sir Frederick, ask them to send in some refreshments, would you?'

'Certainly, Ma'am.'

'He's a good man,' Queen Victoria said, once her private secretary had left the room, 'a very good man indeed, but a little stuffy. He takes his work too seriously. We will have a much more intimate conversation by ourselves.'

Nathaniel nodded. He had no idea what he ought to say next. Then he remembered his grandfather's advice and he waited for the Queen to speak to him.

She began by asking him how he was enjoying living with his grandfather.

'Very well, Ma'am,' he told her.

'It must be a very different life from the one you had been used to.'

'Very different indeed.'

'We have been told that your father was

a practising medium.'

Nathaniel hesitated. 'Not really,' he said.

'Explain.'

'He was a fraud, Ma'am. It was all an act.'

The Queen frowned. 'All an act?' she said.

'My father only pretended to communicate with the dead. He had an accomplice who found out things about the people who came to the seances and he used those details to make it look as though he was receiving messages.'

Queen Victoria appeared deeply shocked.

'You say your father took money from these people?'

'Yes, Ma'am.'

She was silent for a long time. Finally she said, 'We are most sorry to hear of this, Master Wolfe,'

'Yes, Ma'am.'

At that moment what Nathaniel wished most dearly was for the ground to open up and swallow him. Instead there was a knock on the door and a servant appeared carrying a tray laden with tea and cakes. The Queen waited in silence while the tea was poured out.

'Milk and sugar, Master Wolfe?' she asked.

'Just milk, thank you Ma'am,' Nathaniel told her.

She nodded at the servant who poured milk into each cup.

'That will be all, thank you,' she told him.

The servant bowed and exited.

'Would you care for a cake, Master Wolfe?' Queen Victoria went on.

Nathaniel shook his head. 'No thank you, Ma'am.' He didn't trust himself to eat cake with the Queen looking on.

The Queen lifted her cup and sipped her tea. Nathaniel followed suit, conscious that he seemed to drink so much more noisily than she did.

'So your father was a fraudster, Master Wolfe?' the Queen said when she had put her cup down again.

'Yes, Ma'am.'

'And what about you? Are you a fraudster, too?'

'I hope not, Ma'am.'

'Then answer this question truthfully. Can you or can you not communicate with spirits of the dead?'

She was looking at him intently with an expression on her face that he could not entirely fathom. 'The ghost of Mrs Chesterfield appeared to me, Ma'am,' he told her. 'I spoke to her and asked her questions. She said nothing in reply but she did nod. And at times I believe I was able to feel her thoughts.'

Queen Victoria closed her eyes for a moment and let out a long breath, as if she was struggling to keep herself under control. When she opened her eyes again, she leaned forward and spoke in a hushed voice. 'Can you tell whether there are any spirits in the room at this moment?' she asked.

There was something familiar about the way she asked that question, something about the tone of her voice or the look on her face. Then he realised what it was. She shared the same sadness and longing as those who came to Cicero's seances. At last he understood properly why she had sent for him. She hoped that he might be able to bring her a message from Prince Albert.

He opened his mouth to tell her that the room might be filled with dozens of spirits for all he knew, but she was gazing at him with such eagerness that he hated to disappoint her. So he hesitated, uncertain what to say next.

'If there is any fee that you require, you have only to name it,' she told him.

This, then, was what his father had felt. This same sense of need and an awareness of the power that came from it. He had only to tell the Queen that he could see a gentleman with a black moustache and a regal bearing standing directly behind her – and that the gentleman wanted her to know that she should not worry because he was watching over her and waiting to meet her again – and he would make her happy for the rest of her life.

More than that, he realised. He would become

the Queen's special friend. Even Sir Frederick Ponsonby would have to look up to him. Nathaniel and Queen Victoria would agree that Sir Frederick was good at his job but a bit of a bore, lacking in imagination. Perhaps Prince Albert might even share this opinion. Nathaniel could imagine himself telling the Queen that her husband was far from certain about her private secretary. And Sir Frederick would have to mind his Ps and Qs.

What influence he could have! He would only have to tell her that Prince Albert thought something would be a good idea and it would be carried out immediately. Those who wanted favours would have to come to him first and win his approval. The thought of it was dizzying.

'Well, Master Wolfe?' the Queen persisted. 'Have you nothing to say to me?'

But there was no choice, really. Nathaniel was not going to turn out like his father. He shook his head. 'I'm sorry, Your Majesty,' he said. 'I've only ever seen one spirit and I didn't want to see her, really.'

Queen Victoria nodded sadly and sank back in her chair like a balloon that had been punctured. 'It was too much to hope for,' she said, speaking almost to herself. Not long afterwards she got up from her chair and pulled a bell cord.

A moment later Sir Frederick Ponsonby returned.

'Our audience with Master Wolfe has come to an end,' she told him. 'It was most enjoyable, but a little tiring.'

Nathaniel bowed and followed Sir Frederick out of the room.

'I trust you remembered my advice,' Sir Frederick said as he led the way back along the red-carpeted corridor.

'It wasn't necessary, thank you,' Nathaniel told him.

Sir Frederick frowned and opened his mouth to say something further but Nathaniel stopped him. 'Actually, I have some advice for you,' he said.

'Advice for me?' Sir Frederick looked astonished.

'I think you take your work too seriously,' Nathaniel told him. 'You're a good man, but a little bit stuffy.'

19. FREE AND EASY

'I can understand exactly how the poor woman felt,' Mr Monkton said when Nathaniel described his interview with the Queen. 'After your grandmother's death I was ready to clutch at any straw that was offered to me.'

'Is that why you wrote to my father?' Nathaniel asked.

Mr Monkton shook his head. 'I had made up my mind to write even before poor Mary became sick. If anything, her illness only postponed the letter. You see I finally understood that in rejecting your father I had made a terrible mistake, one for which our whole family has paid the price. It was up to me, therefore, to make amends. I thank God that you were able to read that letter and we have all been given a second chance. For my part, I do not intend to waste that opportunity. Others must do as they think fit. Now, are you ready for your next encounter?'

'Yes, I am,' Nathaniel replied.

'Good. You realise that this may be much harder than your interview with the Queen.'

Nathaniel nodded.

'Very well. Let us waste no further time.'

They left the inn and set off once more in a hansom cab. But this journey was very different from the one that Nathaniel had taken earlier in the day. Instead of getting wider and smarter, the streets through which they travelled grew narrower and more shabby at every turn. Instead of grander houses, they passed block after block of slum dwellings. Soon they were in territory that was completely familiar to Nathaniel – the East End of London. At last they pulled up outside Mrs Bizzantine's boarding house, where Jeremiah stood waiting for them dressed in his Sunday best.

He grinned at them opened the carriage door and climbed inside. 'Evening, Mr Monkton,' he said.

'Good evening, Jeremiah. You are all set for this evening's adventure?'

'I reckon I am, sir.'

'Splendid.' Mr Monkton leaned out of the window and gave the driver the signal to set off again.

'Well, Nathaniel,' Jeremiah said. 'It seems you've become a proper gentleman.'

'I'm still the same person I always was,' Nathaniel assured him.

Jeremiah shook his head. 'The famous Master Nathaniel Wolfe,' he said. 'I've been hearing your name everywhere I go. I'm quite a celebrity myself on account of getting mixed up with you.'

'You don't regret it, do you?

Jeremiah tapped his nose with his forefinger. 'Course not. I've put the price of my rats up on account of it.'

'That reminds me,' Mr Monkton said. 'I have a proposition to put to you, Jeremiah.'

'I'm all ears, Mr Monkton.'

'As you may be aware, I have a very small estate in Kent,' Mr Monkton went on. 'A few acres, no more, laid out in lawns and gardens. Now my gardener, Abraham, is an old man who is reaching retirement, and I wondered whether you might like to take the job on? There would be no heavy work, I can assure you. That would all be done by your assistants. And while I can only guess at the financial reward you receive from your current employment, I feel sure that the remuneration in your new post would be significantly greater. So, what do you say?'

It was a plan that Mr Monkton and Nathaniel had discussed at length on the journey down to London and now they both looked towards Jeremiah in pleasurable anticipation of his acceptance. But, to their surprise, he shook his head.

'It's very handsome of you, Mr Monkton, very handsome indeed. And I do appreciate it. But with regret I must decline your offer.'

'You'd rather continue working down the sewers?' Mr Monkton asked in astonishment.

'As it happens, Mr Monkton, I would. I know that must seem very strange to a gentleman such as yourself but I'm a tosher, see. Born and bred. And the sewers is my world. Now if I was to suddenly find myself in another world, I'd be like a fish out of water. Wagging my tail and gasping for breath. I wouldn't know which way to turn, sir. So if it's all the same to you, I'll stick with what I know.'

'Of course,' Mr Monkton agreed, reluctantly. 'But if you should change your mind, you have only to come and find me.'

By now they were passing over London Bridge and, down below, the River Thames moved sluggishly, its waters grown thick and heavy with the waste and filth of the city. It was a windless night and the stench was bad enough to make Mr Monkton pull his scarf over his face.

Seeing this, Jeremiah grinned. 'You'll never make a Londoner, sir,' he said.

'I'm afraid you're right,' Mr Monkton agreed. 'I cannot wait to return to the clean air of the countryside. It is only the importance of our errand this evening that makes me linger in this dreadful place.'

There was silence as both Nathaniel and his grandfather brooded over what lay ahead of them. Only Jeremiah remained relaxed as the cab driver picked his way through the narrow streets beneath a dark and threatening sky.

At last they pulled up outside a tavern. Mr Monkton paid the cab driver while Nathaniel and Jeremiah stood gazing at a billboard that had been plastered to the wall.

'Ladies and gentlemen,' Nathaniel read aloud, 'you are invited to step inside for an evening of fun, frolics and feasting. We guarantee that you will not be disappointed.'

'That's quite a promise,' Jeremiah observed.

Nathaniel nodded, too nervous to reply.

They opened the doors of the inn and immediately a great wave of beer-soaked, gin-smelling, pie-flavoured air burst upon them. Stepping inside, they found themselves in a large low-ceilinged room with rows of tables down the sides and middle, and a raised platform at one end that served as a stage. The place was filled with a vast crowd of people, some respectable, some less so, all of them enthusiastically consuming large quantities of food and drink while sweating waiters and waitresses hurried back and forth between the tables carrying trays piled high with mugs of ale and dishes of mutton stew.

Amid the general hubbub it was scarcely possible to make yourself heard but Jeremiah pointed to an empty table in one corner and they squeezed through the throng towards it. No sooner had they sat down than a gentleman with enormous side whiskers, dressed in a canary-yellow waistcoat and a top hat, appeared on the stage and announced, to cheers and whistles from the audience, that the evening's entertainment was about to begin. 'So, ladies and gentleman,' he declared, 'prepare to make yourselves free and easy and enjoy the show.'

An extraordinary collection of performers followed each other onto the stage over the next hour or so. There was a man who juggled with knives, a clown with a trio of performing dogs, a Scotsman in a kilt who sang ballads about the glens of his homeland and a one-legged trumpet player. But finally the moment that Nathaniel and his grandfather had been waiting for arrived. The master of ceremonies announced that he was proud to introduce the melodious and mellifluous Mister Henry Wolfe, and the Shadwell Nightingale, Mrs Agatha Gaunt. While the crowd clapped enthusiastically and banged their mugs on the tables, Nathaniel glanced at his grandfather to see how he was taking it, but Mr Monkton's face revealed nothing.

Henry and Agatha walked out onto the stage and Nathaniel bit his lip. Had he been asked what he had expected before setting out that evening, he could not exactly have said. But he knew what he dreaded – a terrible performance, the jeers of the audience and a hasty retreat from the stage. For even though his father had abandoned him, Nathaniel did not want to see him publicly ridiculed.

But he need not have worried. Henry and Agatha were a great deal better than he had expected. They began with a comic song about a rat-catcher's daughter from Westminster that made the audience, particularly Jeremiah, laugh out loud and stamp their feet with delight. Then they sang a number of serious songs which were politely received, finishing off with the tale of a farmer visiting London for the very first time. It had a rousing chorus that the audience joined in with enthusiastically.

'Well, Nathaniel,' Mr Monkton said when the act was finished, 'it seems your father has more talent than I had imagined. Now, however, I think it is time we went and had a word with him.'

Nathaniel nodded and they got up together, leaving Jeremiah to enjoy the rest of the show. They made their way over to the door at the side of the stage from which the various performers had appeared. It opened on to a long, narrow room crowded with artists in the process of getting ready. And there at one end of the room were Henry, formerly Cicero, Wolfe and Agatha Gaunt, looking not at all displeased with themselves.

Henry's face changed dramatically, however, when he caught sight of Nathaniel and his grandfather. It was clear that he had not expected such a visit. Nevertheless, he quickly recovered his composure and turned on Mr Monkton with a sneer. 'You've got a confounded cheek turning up here like this!' he declared. 'And what do you mean by stealing my boy?'

But Mr Monkton was unimpressed by his bluster. 'You abandoned your son,' he pointed out.

'Is that what he told you?' Henry said. He turned to Nathaniel. 'Now you listen to me,' he began.

But Nathaniel had no intention of listening. He had come here to speak for himself and now was the time to do so. He was no longer frightened of his father. Too much had happened since the days when he had been a medium's apprentice. He had faced greater dangers than his father could ever present and he had lived to tell the tale.

'No, you listen to me,' he said. 'I'm living with my grandfather now. He's going to send me to school, which is something you never did. I'm being given a chance to make something of my life and I intend to take it. And that's why I came here to see you, to let you know my decision.'

His father stared back at him open-mouthed.

'Goodbye then,' Nathaniel said. 'I enjoyed your act.' Then he and his grandfather turned and walked away, leaving Henry Wolfe, for perhaps the first and only time in his life, utterly speechless.

There was still one more visit to be made before they could return to Kent, and it took place the following morning. Nathaniel and Mr Monkton arrived at the Chesterfields' house not long after breakfast, where the door was opened to them by Miss Pemberton, Mrs Chesterfield's friend, who was now acting as Sophie's guardian. 'I must carry out the everyday duties of the house until such time as we can get ourselves another maid,' she told them, with a smile.

'I cannot tell you how grateful I am,' she continued when she had shown them both into the front parlour. 'Without the courage that you both showed, Miss Sophie would be lying in the graveyard next to her mother.'

'How is she now?' Mr Monkton asked.

'Just now she is in bed,' Miss Pemberton told them. 'She is still very weak from her ordeal, poor thing. But she grows stronger every day and Lily is a great comfort to her. Why, here she is!'

Lily stood in the doorway beaming at Nathaniel. 'I thought you'd forgotten all about me,' she told him.

'Of course not!' he said. 'There's just been so much to do.'

'Come on upstairs,' she said. 'Sophie is very anxious to see you. She never stops asking me about you.'

Nathaniel looked at his grandfather, who nodded. 'By all means,' he said. 'You young people have a great deal to talk about. Miss Pemberton and I will do very nicely by ourselves.'

'What's it like being the grandson of a gentleman?' Lily asked, as she led the way.

Nathaniel shrugged. 'A bit strange at first, but I'm starting to get used to it. What's it like being Sophie's companion instead of a housemaid?'

Lily laughed. 'It sounds so strange not calling her Miss Sophie but I suppose I shall get used to it. Not everyone's entirely pleased with the arrangement, though,' she went on. 'Mrs Simpson has had her nose thoroughly put out of joint, I can tell you. I heard her saying to George that she never expected to be receiving orders from a housemaid. And as for George himself... Well, he doesn't know what to do when he sees me. Scuttles away like a spider in a woodshed.'

'I expect he'll come round in time,' Nathaniel told her.

They were standing outside Sophie's bedroom now and Lily rapped on the door with her knuckles before pushing it open. Sophie was sitting up in bed and she looked delighted to see them. Though still pale and worn-looking, she was clearly much better. She thanked Nathaniel so many times for what he had done that he had to threaten to leave immediately if she did not stop.

She wanted to hear everything that had happened, even though she had already heard Lily's side of the story a dozen times. But after a while she became tired and Lily and Nathaniel left her to rest.

'You won't forget about us, now that you're living in the country?' Lily said as they went back downstairs.

'Of course not,' Nathaniel told her.

'Promise?'

'I promise. Besides, I've got a feeling about us,' he went on.

'What sort of a feeling?'

'It's hard to describe. I just think that there might be more things we have to do together, people we need to help.'

'What on earth makes you say that?'

Nathaniel shrugged. 'Just a hunch, I suppose.

I was sitting on the train on the way down to London and it came into my mind.'

'Well, just so long as it doesn't involve any more ghosts,' Lily said.

Nathaniel opened his mouth to reply but just then his grandfather came out into the hall. 'I think we had best be on our way,' he said.

The hansom was waiting outside, so they said their goodbyes and climbed on board. Mr Monkton settled back in his seat with a sigh of contentment, but Nathaniel leaned out of the window, looking back at the house with a feeling of regret. And that was when he saw Mrs Chesterfield once more. She was standing at one of the upstairs windows, staring directly at him with those eyes that seemed to look right into his soul. She raised her hand in farewell and Nathaniel waved back. Then she vanished, and the cab pulled away.

Coming soon…

Look out for the second Nathaniel Wolfe adventure

For more information about Brian Keaney and the books he writes, log on to www.briankeaney.com

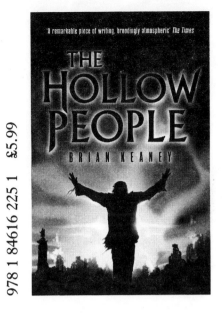

978 1 84616 225 1   £5.99

On the island of Tarnagar is an asylum where
you can be locked up for dreaming. Dante
works in the kitchen and Bea is the privileged
daughter of doctors. When their worlds collide,
they are forced to confront the extraordinary
evil lurking behind Dr Sigmundus, the ruler of
their nation.

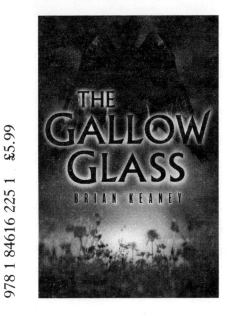

978 1 84616 225 1 · £5.99

Dante is on the run, Bea is in prison and Ezekiel is wounded. Things do not look good for the Púca, the tiny band of individuals who refuse to accept the authority of Dr Sigmundus. And they're about to get a whole lot worse.

In the depths of the Odyll a new kind of evil is about to be born. Its name is Gallowglass and its mission is simple. Hunt down and destroy those who will not obey. Only Dante can stop it. To do so he must face a terrible choice and discover the dark secret at the heart of his own family.

OTHER ORCHARD BOOKS YOU MAY ENJOY

The Fire Within	Chris d'Lacey	978 1 84121 533 4
Icefire	Chris d'Lacey	978 1 84362 134 8
Fire Star	Chris d'Lacey	978 1 84362 522 3
The Fire Eternal	Chris d'Lacey	978 1 84616 426 2
The Truth Cookie	Fiona Dunbar	978 1 84362 549 0
Cupid Cakes	Fiona Dunbar	978 1 84362 688 6
Chocolate Wishes	Fiona Dunbar	978 1 84362 689 3
Toonhead	Fiona Dunbar	978 1 84616 238 1
Pink Chameleon	Fiona Dunbar	978 1 84616 230 5
Blue Gene Baby	Fiona Dunbar	978 1 84616 231 2

All priced at £5.99

Orchard Red Apples are available from all good bookshops,
or can be ordered direct from the publisher:
Orchard Books, PO BOX 29, Douglas IM99 1BQ
Credit card orders please telephone 01624 836000
or fax 01624 837033 or visit our website: www.orchardbooks.co.uk
or e-mail: bookshop@enterprise.net for details.

To order please quote title, author and ISBN
and your full name and address.
Cheques and postal orders should be made payable to 'Bookpost plc.'
Postage and packing is FREE within the UK
(overseas customers should add £1.00 per book).

Prices and availability are subject to change.